A THOUSAND MILES AWAY

After her father remarried, Farrell's stepmother had made it clear that she wasn't
welcome at home any more. So Farrell
took herself off and bravely tried to find
another life of her own. But, for reasons of
his own, the masterful Larry Sandfort kept
following her and bringing her back.
Would Farrell never manage to get away
from him?

A THOUSAND MILES AWAY

BY

DOROTHY CORK

MILLS & BOON LIMITED
17–19 FOLEY STREET
LONDON W1A 1DR

First published 1978
Australian copyright 1978
Philippine copyright 1978
This edition 1978

© Dorothy Cork 1978

ISBN 0 263 72691 6

Set in Linotype Plantin 10 on 11 pt.

Made and printed in Great Britain by
Richard Clay (The Chaucer Press), Ltd., Bungay, Suffolk

wearing now. Farrell admired her for her vivacity, and for the creativity she displayed in the pictures she made from her beach garnerings. But the fact was, they weren't getting on.

She told Farrell tightly, once Larry Sandfort was out of earshot, 'If you're so determined to make yourself useful in the restaurant this evening, Farrell, it surprises me you didn't run off to shower and make yourself respectable instead of wandering over here so nosily to play chaperone to me.'

Colour surged into Farrell's cheeks and her grey-green eyes darkened.

'I didn't mean it that way, Cecile. It was just that Mr Sandfort saw me and smiled, and I thought he wanted me to—to——'

'Now why should you think he wanted you to do anything? You're here at your own invitation, and no one else's. Larry Sandfort is a mature man, Farrell—a very mature man. The company of a girl not yet twenty who's had practically no experience of life beyond what she's gained in a girls' school is hardly likely to hold him spellbound. Now is it?'

'No. I'm—sorry,' Farrell said with a sigh, and half rose from her chair. But at that moment Larry Sandfort came back with the drinks, and she subsided again.

'Cheers!' he said, taking a chair between the two women and raising his glass of beer. Cecile was all sparkles again. 'Cheers!' she echoed, and Farrell murmured the word too. She had better get rid of her drink quickly and make her departure, she decided, and was disconcerted when Larry Sandfort said, 'Well, Farrell, let's hear something about you. Your father tells me you suddenly took it into your head to quit university. What was it? The lure of the North-West?'

'The lure of the relaxed life!' Cecile exclaimed before

Farrell had a chance to answer. 'A lazy life in her father's wigwam. Though at the moment she's very busily trying to persuade herself—and Tony—that she's indispensable. A bit difficult since he's coped without her help quite adequately for seven or eight years before I came. Of course Farrell thinks I'm an outsider who doesn't understand the way of life here. But I'm from Darwin, Larry—I'm used to the tropics. I've lived in the north all my life.'

The man she addressed listened patiently, and then his blue eyes turned searchingly to Farrell, who sat fingering her glass and feeling rather wretched. She wanted to exclaim that she didn't see Cecile in that light at all, that she was happy her father had married again, yet to protest might sound like starting an argument. She was relieved when Larry Sandfort asked her directly, 'Helping at the hotel apart, what's your immediate object, then, Farrell?'

This time Farrell answered before Cecile, whose lips were already parted, could say a word.

'I'm not sure. I just know that university's not for me. I was sort of gently pushed into it. You see, Aunt Jean—I lived with her in Perth after my mother died; Daddy said it was better than being here with him—Aunt Jean and my mother were sisters, and she's a lecturer at the University of Western Australia—terribly keen and clever. She put it into my head when I was about twelve and somehow or other topped the class—the only time I ever did, or even came near it—that I was a Roseblade. That's my mother's family. They were all rather bookish, except Mummy, though she just loved reading.' She paused, aware that Cecile had raised her eyes skywards and was looking bored, and plainly suggesting by doing so that the man of the party was sure to be bored too. Farrell sipped her drink and looked at him quickly over her glass, met his eyes and glanced away as she encountered his searching regard.

'Carry on,' he prompted when she didn't resume. 'What

happened? You must have passed your exams quite well to have gained a place at university.'

'Yes, but I had to work so terribly hard!' Farrell said with a grimace. 'You've got no idea. It didn't come easily. I spent all my time studying—I had this awful feeling that I just had to come up to her expectations. And Daddy was so proud of me,' she added. 'But I really wasn't being true to myself—I was trying to—to duplicate my aunt.' She turned her gaze to his face again to see if he was looking as sceptical as Cecile was, or if he looked as if he knew what she meant. She couldn't tell, even though he nodded. 'Well, then I had the 'flu. And while I was sick I had time to do a lot of thinking, and I—I reached the conclusion I'd been trying to set myself in the wrong mould. It was a—hard decision to make, Aunt Jean was so terribly disappointed, but I made up my mind to leave university and start anew. I'd always loved coming back home, so it was the natural place to begin. And here I am!'

'And that is the story of Farrell's life,' said Cecile. Her voice was light, but the expression on it was dampening. 'Hard work—rebellion—escape. Now she's a thousand miles away from reality.'

'It's not escape from reality,' Farrell protested. 'I've talked to Daddy about it, and he sympathises.'

'He's soft-hearted,' Cecile said flatly. 'It may be unpalatable to you, Farrell, but it's a simple case of rejecting responsibility. You've come home because it's so much easier than battling for a place in the world. What you don't realise is that it's the struggle, the effort, the acceptance of responsibility that give value to life and achievement.'

'I do realise that—I do,' Farrell insisted, her cheeks flushed. She felt a little embarrassed to be involved in this personal kind of near-wrangling in the presence of a stranger. 'But the point is, it's stupid to struggle to achieve the wrong end, to work madly to fit yourself for a—a life that doesn't suit you. I don't want everything made easy. I've said I'll do anything here that's asked of me—I'll clean the rooms, help in the kitchen—anything!'

'Oh, for goodness' sake!' Cecile exclaimed impatiently. 'You know your father won't ask that of you. He doesn't need to. The hotel has come a long way since you lived here as a little girl—it's developing very fast into a holiday resort. But all this is very boring for Mr Sandfort——'

Mr Sandfort didn't contradict that statement. Instead he asked Farrell, 'You do have some idea about your future, Farrell, I take it?'

Farrell hadn't really—and she hated to admit it. She had very vague ideas of writing—so vague, so new, so uncertain, she hadn't mentioned them even to her father, let alone to Cecile. The only person she had mentioned them to, in fact, was Mark Smith, a boy she met sometimes on the beach. He and she had something in common in that they were both trying to discover where they belonged. He worked on the prawning trawlers along the coast at the moment, and was not very much older than she was. To him, Farrell had recited some snippets of poetry she had composed since coming to the North-West, and though he had listened, she didn't think he had been particularly impressed. English was one of her interests—but it wasn't one of his.

Now, though she hadn't meant to admit to it, something in the way Larry Sandfort was looking at her, expectantly, interestedly, made her tell him, 'I think I might like to be a writer.'

Cecile laughed aloud. 'A writer! That's something new!' She crinkled her eyes. 'Oh, Farrell! You a writer! What on earth would you have to write about at nineteen—and with your dismally limited experience?'

Farrell felt herself curl up inside at the mockery in that voice. She wished she had said nothing at all, because there was no answer to what Cecile had said, except to remind her that her experience wasn't going to be widened very much if she continued to live with her aunt as she had been doing—in a world where books meant more than people. An ivory tower suited her aunt, but Farrell had begun to discover restlessly that it didn't really suit her. She longed to be free of the influence of Aunt Jean's views on sex—to form her own ideas. But freeing herself was not easy after several years of blind belief. 'Sex is brutish and a bore,' Aunt Jean had said. 'I'd sooner find my pleasure in reading some of Shakespeare's sonnets any day.' That had seemed very fine and idealistic to Farrell at fifteen, and it had coloured her outlook to such an extent that she had gained a reputation for being a prig and a cold frog, as someone had once put it. That hurt, but boys were very much inclined to leave Farrell Fitzgerald to her own devices—and to her books. The walls, in fact, had been closing in . . .

'Experience,' she heard Larry Sandfort say, 'comes with the years.' She didn't look at him but finished her gin squash quickly and prepared to take her departure. 'I'm afraid I can't give you any advice about writing, Farrell, but I do know that if you want anything badly enough, you have a pretty good chance of attaining it. Most desires and ambitions have their roots in dreams and grow from there.'

Farrell stood up nervously, and he got to his feet too. She wondered if she should thank him for treating her seriously, for not laughing at her, but she was still smarting from Cecile's scorn, and she merely nodded and said, 'I'll have to go now. Thank you for the drink, Mr Sandfort.'

'I've enjoyed your company,' he said, and she met his eyes briefly again before she moved quickly away.

She encountered her father at the arched gateway, overgrown with scarlet bougainvillea, in the wall that enclosed the swimming pool and terrace.

'Have you had a nice swim, darling?' he asked her.

'Yes, thanks, Daddy. I'm going to shower now, and when I'm dressed I'll come and help with the smorgasbord.' She smiled at him and he smiled back. He was a heavily built man with a muscular neck and massive shoulders. His short cut hair was beginning to show some silver, and his eyes were the same colour as his daughter's. He wasn't particularly tall—not as tall as Larry Sandfort, for instance—but Farrell remembered him, when she was a child, using his bulk to quell the disreputable element that had sometimes erupted at the hotel in those days. Things had changed since then. Not long after she had been sent to Perth, the hotel had been almost entirely destroyed by a cyclone. Tony had rebuilt it on more modern lines, and the tourist trade had increased as the North-West became slightly more accessible. The tone of the place had lifted and now it had a growing reputation as a resort, and was known as well for the excellence of the meals it offered, for Tony had been fortunate to secure a good chef, whom he paid well. A smorgasbord was served on four nights of the week, and the tables in the big dining room, as well as those in its small annexes, were always crowded. Farrell loved the atmosphere on those nights, and she loved being in the dining room and hearing the guests praise the beautifully set out and lavish buffet of seafoods, cold meats, salads and sauces.

But now her father told her briefly, 'Darling, you don't have to help in the dining room——'

'Oh, but I love to help,' she exclaimed. 'I haven't come home just to sit around and enjoy the sun and be lazy.'

'I know that, Farrell.' His smile had vanished. 'All the same, the privilege of presiding at the smorgasbord belongs to Cecile. I appreciate your wanting to help of course, but I'd sooner you found something where you're not—er—treading on anyone's toes.'

'Have I been doing that?' Farrell stared at him appalled. 'I—I had no idea. I thought—well, there was no one there that first night, so I just naturally——'

'Cecile was a few minutes late,' her father said slowly. 'We don't work strictly to the clock——' His gaze shifted and he smiled over her shoulder, and Farrell turned her head to see Cecile and Larry Sandfort approaching.

She said quickly, 'I'm sorry, Daddy. I'll try to be more—more tactful in the future—not to tread on any toes. Of course it's Cecile's right to preside. I just didn't think. I shan't—intrude again.'

'Good,' he said. By now the others were within speaking distance, and though Farrell had turned away and was making rapidly for the wing where her room was, Cecile's voice reached her ears.

'Has Farrell been telling tales?'

Farrell didn't hear her father's answer, but her cheeks burned. It hurt that Cecile should have asked that question —as if she, Farrell, were out to make mischief, when that was the last thing she wanted to do.

She showered, dressed neatly in beige pants and a peacock green shirt, then, as she brushed her hair at the mirror, suddenly longed for someone to talk to. Not necessarily about the things that were bothering her, such as her failure to get on with Cecile, her failure to work out a definite future for herself—but just to talk to. Not Aunt Jean, who couldn't be bothered with small talk anyhow, and not any other person in particular either. She missed ridiculously the affectionate letters her father used to write her so regularly when she was a thousand miles away in Perth. She had been closer to him then than she was now, when she stopped to think about it. She had had only one long heart-to-heart talk with him since she had come home, and that had been on the day she arrived. Since then, she had realised that now he had a wife, her position was a secondary one. She had done her best to accept that, and been glad for her father that he was happy, but there was still this gap in her life.

Farrell had intended to wander round the bar and see if

she could give a hand there, but instead she skirted the wall that enclosed the terrace and climbed into the sandhills behind the hotel. Coarse grey-green grasses bonded the sand, and the wind blew in from the Indian Ocean. She stood looking down on to the long white beach and the dark lines and scattering of shells and seaweed and broken coral that the big tides brought in. The sea was lazy this evening, its jewel colours softening as the sun went down in the cloudless sky, and the beach was almost deserted. A girl lay asleep, face down, a middle-aged couple were picking over a heap of sea litter, and some distance away a young man in rolled-up jeans wandered on his own. Farrell's heart leapt hopefully, and she ran down the long slope towards the sea.

But it wasn't Mark, and with a sigh, she wandered slowly and lonely along the hard white sand where the tide was receding. Her thoughts were troubled, she felt aimless, useless, and as well she was hungry. Perhaps she had made a mistake in deciding to leave Perth so precipitately. Her aunt had been—not exactly hurt, because she was a very controlled unemotional woman—but she had felt let down. It wasn't too late to go back, of course, yet Farrell knew she simply couldn't. It had taken her a long time to realise that she did have a choice, that there was an alternative to following in Aunt Jean's footsteps; that what her aunt decreed for her was not necessarily what she wanted herself, and didn't have to be accepted.

Yet what had she exchanged that ordered life *for*? Cecile had merely been stating facts when she had said Farrell wasn't needed at the hotel. As for her assertion that she wanted to be a writer—once again her stepmother had stated facts. She hadn't had anything like enough experience of life to write anything worth while. She just liked playing with words—though she hadn't played with them all that much. She was honest enough to admit to herself that the idea of writing might be just a sort of—excuse. What had that Sandfort man said? If you want anything badly enough, you have a good chance of achieving it. Farrell knew she didn't want to write nearly badly enough.

He—Larry Sandfort—had been quite pleasant, she mused. Quite understanding. Unexpectedly understanding, in fact, she thought, as, head down, she tramped along in the sand. Had there been a—a sympathy between them? Or had he really been bored, and hiding it? And *had* he meant her to come over to their table and have a drink with him and Cecile?

'Perhaps I behaved badly,' Farrell thought worriedly. She wasn't really very clued up when it came to relating to other people, thanks to the very limited social life she had led in Perth. For all she knew she had blundered there just as badly as she had blundered in taking over Cecile's place at the smorgasbord. Perhaps Cecile had wanted Larry Sandfort to herself. Even married women of thirty-nine must enjoy a harmless flirtation, Farrell reflected. But would flirting with a man like Larry Sandfort be all that harmless? She didn't know why she suspected that it would not. Perhaps it was something to do with the effect those blue eyes of his had on her. As if they were communicating some message that she, less than a year out of school, was incapable of interpreting.

She thought of Mark, long-haired, casual, not much of a talker, not in the least like Larry Sandfort. She sensed no danger in her association with *him*. He had kissed her a few times, and she had steeled herself not to resist; that puritanical idealism she had caught from Aunt Jean had to be overcome. Nevertheless, she hadn't enjoyed Mark's kisses, though she thought she had hidden that from him quite successfully, and she was sure it must simply be a matter of getting used to such physical contact. A couple of days ago, things had gone a little further. She had fallen asleep on the sand, and Mark had found her there and tickled her nose with a bit of dry seaweed. She woke and they had wrestled together, but she had got away. He had chased her as far as the sandhills and then she had sought refuge in the hotel grounds. He wouldn't follow her there and she knew it. He had come to the hotel only once, and she had introduced him to Cecile. He refused to come again. 'All those tourists and holidaymakers get on my nerves,' was his only excuse.

Mark had cleared out from his father's sheep station somewhere in the Pilbara. 'I was being pushed around like a kid by my father,' was all he told Farrell. 'If you want to do your own thing you have to get right away from family interference. It's the only way to become independent.'

Farrell too wanted to do her own thing, but she had come back to her father's home to try to find her feet. And it wasn't working out ...

The sky was beginning to darken when she turned back along the beach, and though she felt hungry, she didn't hurry. It wasn't like going back to the happy home she had envisaged when she had packed her bags and flown out of Perth. Not at all. It was practically dark and she had started to climb the sandhills when she almost ran into Larry Sandfort. She knew instinctively it was he, and he apparently recognised her as instantaneously.

'Hello, it's you, Farrell! I was on my way to look for you. You haven't eaten, have you?'

'No,' she said uncertainly. They had stopped within a foot of each other, and she was once again impressed by his size.

'I expected to find you in the dining room,' he remarked. 'What happened? Mrs Fitzgerald was a bit put out at having to take over herself.'

Farrell bit her lip. It seemed you couldn't win. She had thought she was doing the right thing in disappearing after what her father had said. She hoped there hadn't been friction between Cecile and Tony because he had put her off.

'Nothing happened,' she said helplessly. 'I just—changed my mind.' It was hardly the whole truth, but she didn't feel inclined to explain the touchy relationship that had grown up between herself and her stepmother.

'Perhaps that wasn't a good idea under the circumstances,' he commented. 'Well, I haven't eaten either. I think the best plan might be for us to go to that restaurant in town—what's its name? The Lobster Pot?'

Farrell felt slightly stunned. Was he inviting her to eat with him or was she going off her head?

She said confusedly, 'The seafood there isn't nearly as good as ours——'

'I daresay not. But as I'm more interested in you than in food—and I hope the same goes for you—and as you can eat at the Coral Reef any night of the week, it surely doesn't matter all that much. Are you wearing sandals or thongs, by the way?'

'Sandals,' she said with a slight quaver. He *was* inviting her to eat with him and it was totally incomprehensible, and even apart from that she was so hungry she could hardly think straight. But at least she understood his question. All reputable eating places up here had a rule that people wearing thongs, or without a shirt, did not eat on their premises. Farrell felt a little relieved that she didn't have to go back to the hotel and face Cecile, yet—why should this man want to take her out to dinner? Already he had taken her arm and they were moving towards the hotel.

'Why—why are you taking me to dinner?' she managed to ask as he guided her through the grounds to where his car was parked.

'Why do you think?' He opened the door for her, saw her seated, slammed the door shut, and in a moment was seated beside her. 'Why does a man generally ask a woman to dine with him?' he resumed.

'I—I have no idea,' Farrell said naïvely.

'You haven't?' He sounded really amused. 'Well, let's say it's so we can talk.' He started up the motor and as the car moved forward, she asked:

'What—what do you want to talk to me about?'

'Various things,' he said. 'A lot of things. Far too many things for the time at our disposal, in fact. I'm afraid I have to leave in the morning.'

'Tomorrow? Already? You only came yesterday,' she exclaimed, turning her head to stare at his dark, unfamiliar profile.

'Yes. But I've done what I came here to do—a little bit of private investigation. I didn't count on meeting you. And unfortunately I have some urgent business to see to on the tableland, and in two days' time I must be in Perth.'

'Oh. Your work has something to do with iron ore mining, hasn't it?' Farrell, quite unnerved by his remark about meeting her, hardly knew what she was saying.

'Well, how did you know that?' He sounded mildly surprised.

'What? Oh, my father told me.'

'Was it information given gratuitously or asked for?'

'I—I asked him.'

'Why did you do that?'

She shrugged in the dark of the car. 'I don't know—I just wondered, I guess.'

He laughed. 'I was hoping for a compliment. Still, at least you asked.'

Farrell was silent. She hadn't the least idea what this was all about. Neither of them said anything further until in not many minutes they reached the tiny town where the Lobster Pot was. Farrell had actually never been to this restaurant before, she had merely heard her father and Cecile dis-

cussing the food there. It was attractive enough, unpretenti-
ous, licensed. Taped music provided a background to conversation, and there were pretty and unsophisticated girls
waiting on the tables. A quick look around assured Farrell
that she didn't look out of place in the clothes she was
wearing, and she had run a comb through her hair in the
car, feeling thankful she carried one in the pocket of her
pants.

Larry ordered wine first of all and then with the remark,
'You haven't been here so long you're sated by seafood, I
take it?' he ordered crayfish and a salad for them both.
Farrell sat blinking in the rather dim pinkish light, feeling
that somehow everything had suddenly been turned upside
down or inside out, and that her life was going to be given a
new twist. This was the first time since she had left Perth
that she had dined anywhere other than at her father's
hotel. It was the first time in her life that she had eaten
alone with a man, apart from her father.

She glanced through her lashes at the man sitting opposite her and presently engaged in pouring wine into her
glass. Who would ever have believed she'd be eating out
with *him* tonight! He was really rather—impressive. He
wore a dark brown long-sleeved shirt, and she noticed the
disconcerting cleft in a chin that was otherwise aggressive.
His eyes, when he raised them suddenly to meet hers, were
quizzical, and almost dazzlingly blue. What on earth could
he want to talk to her about?

He raised his glass. 'Well, let's hear some more about
you, Farrell.'

'Me?' Her bewilderment was obvious. She took a quick
swallow of her wine, a very light rosé.

'Yes. You've opted out of city life to come back here
where people are warm and friendly and relaxed. Or can
be, should I say?' he amended wryly, and she wondered if
he were thinking of Cecile as he said it.

'Yes,' she murmured vaguely.

'What's brushed off on you from the company you mixed with in Perth?'

'I—I don't know what you mean,' she stammered. Colour stained her cheeks as, madly, into her mind came the voice of Penny Watson, telling her, 'My brother says you're as cold as a frog'.

'I'm thinking of Women's Lib—that's rife in university circles,' he said after a moment. He moved his elbow off the table as the waitress brought the dishes he had ordered. There was a pause while they helped themselves to salad, started on the crayfish, then he gave her one of his frankly searching looks. 'Have you been brainwashed with a lot of ideas on the subject by—members of the club, Farrell? Or have you managed to keep out of all that?'

'I've kept out of it,' she said. Oh, how she'd kept out of it! Surely no one could have been more untouched by Women's Lib than Farrell Fitzgerald.

'I thought as much,' he said, and added, 'I hope you don't object if we begin to talk about love—or sex—over the crayfish? We don't have all that much time.'

'I—don't mind,' Farrell said awkwardly. She glanced around her, at other tables where people were talking, laughing, drinking, eating—young people, middle-aged people, elderly people. She and the man opposite her were surely no different from the rest—well, she amended that thought, no one else in the room had his charisma, but this conversation—where was it all leading? Hungry as she was, she tried to give her full attention to the crayfish, but somehow failed, commendable though it was. She felt almost transfixed by the man she was dining with.

He looked across at her, his eyes glinting. 'I rather think you have a nice clean slate, Farrell. I'd like to write something on it—something important.'

'What?' she asked, staring, not understanding what he was getting at.

He laid down his fork and looked at her bemusedly, his eyes travelling from her fair hair to her soft, rather wide mouth.

'Well, this for a start. That the love relationship between a man and woman is the most important thing in life.'

Farrell stared and listened and repeated it in her mind. The love relationship between a man and a woman—— Was he—could he be—talking about her father and Cecile? Warning her in some way about not upsetting the relationship between Tony and his new wife? Or was he talking about himself? They had talked about her this evening, she reflected, taking another sip of the rosé, but they had not talked about him.

'Are you married, Mr Sandfort?' she asked interestedly.

He laughed. 'Farrell, you are utterly charming and totally incredible. No, I'm thirty-five and I'm not married. But I've loved and lost a sufficient number of times to learn that life without love, without a woman who is part of you physically and emotionally and mentally, is as barren as the desert.'

Yes, Farrell thought, he was probably right. This very evening, because she had had no one to talk to, *her* life had begun to feel as empty as a desert. She nodded soberly, and he said with a slightly sad crooked smile that did something to her heart, 'You don't really know anything about it yet, do you? You're possibly more concerned with this idea of yours to become a writer.'

She felt a fraud immediately. 'Not really,' she murmured. She realised it acutely. She was far more concerned with the warmth of human relationships—something that had been missing while she had lived with Jean Roseblade. But of course, she didn't know anything of the kind of love he was talking about.

'No? Well, as I said this afternoon, I couldn't help you there anyway ... Is there a man in your life at this moment?'

Farrell shook her head, and he leaned towards her, pushing his plate aside. 'You're lost, aren't you? You don't know what you're looking for. Am I right?' He paused and she nodded. His next words shocked her. 'Marry me, Farrell. I promise you'll never regret it.'

Farrell was so completely astonished she wondered if she were hearing things—if the rosé had gone to her head. She laid down her fork with a hand that shook.

'Marry you? You—you must be joking!'

'I'm not joking. I'm dead serious,' he said, his blue eyes intent. 'You're in a spot at your father's hotel, Farrell. Do you realise that, or don't you? If you don't watch it—and I'm afraid even if you do watch it—you're going to break up your father's marriage. Maybe you mean well, I'd guess so, but that stepmother of yours doesn't think so. Putting it bluntly, if you love your father, you can't stay around.'

It was a conclusion Farrell was on the way to reaching herself, but she didn't particularly like anyone pointing it out to her. Like Mark, she wanted to work things out for herself. She had followed the guide lines laid down for her by someone else for long enough.

'So,' Larry Sandfort pursued relentlessly, 'marry me.'

'Oh, please——' Farrell pushed her plate aside and her wine glass as well. 'I—I couldn't—I don't know you—people don't do that sort of thing.'

'Don't do it?' His eyebrows rose comically. 'Good God, it's being done constantly. Daily—hourly—people are rushing into marriage with someone they know nothing about. But I didn't mean you and I would do it that way, Farrell. We can do a crash course to learn about each other.'

'How can we?' Farrell protested. 'You're leaving tomorrow. And if you mean——' She stopped, her heart hammering, her cheeks red.

'Now don't jump to conclusions. I don't mean we can do a crash course in bed tonight. I'm not making that kind of proposal, and I don't want to marry you tomorrow. We can learn a lot about each other in a week, and I can manage to free myself for that long. Of course, it would still be asking you to take a drastic step, but if we married before you were completely ready, I'd give you all the time you needed to learn to love me. Don't think I'd ask you to make marriage vows just so that I could have the privilege of going to bed with you. This other thing would work—I could as good as promise you that. Provided we both wanted it to, of course.'

Farrell shook her head. 'How *could* we want it to? I—I couldn't possibly. It's just—well, you can't mean it.'

'I do mean it,' he said, and though his chin was aggressive, the line where his lips met was soft, and there was an expression in his eyes that baffled Farrell and gave her a strange feeling of weakness. 'If you're telling yourself I'm too old for you, that you want a man of twenty-three or four, let me assure you that experience is a help. An older man understands women better—the frictions, the abrasives are missing. I could make your life a Song of Solomon.'

Farrell could only stare at him. She felt almost faint and her senses were reeling. This couldn't be happening to her!

'Now listen, Farrell,' he said quietly after a moment. 'I don't want you to give me an answer now. I've told you I have to go away—for perhaps a couple of weeks. During that time, think about it, will you? Think about me—seriously. When I come back we'll go all out to get to know each other. I promise you can ask me any question you want, however difficult, however personal, and I shall endeavour to answer you with complete honesty. I'd expect the same from you, of course. A week, and we'll know each other a hundred per cent better than the average couple who get married. If sex is worrying you, don't let it. That's a natural part of love—you'd grow towards that.'

'But—but why *me*?' Farrell asked. Her cheeks had

grown pale and she was trembling. The waitress brought coffee, and she began to drink hers, hot, black, unsweetened, as if to clear her brain. It was bitter, and shuddering she reached for the sugar.

'Why you?' he said, as if there had been no interruption. He considered her slowly, from her bright curling hair to her bosom, its soft contour revealed by the silky shirt. His eyes were unfathomable, and Farrell felt a stirring deep within her—a sort of stirring towards knowledge. 'Because I want you,' he said. He spooned sugar into his own coffee, then added deliberately, 'And I'm pushing it because I know you're in a predicament. Your presence here is fouling up your father's marriage. If you're not yet aware of that, you soon will be. Your pretty stepmother doesn't want you around. But perhaps that's your idea—to break the whole thing up? You don't care——'

'I do care,' she said, stung. 'I love my father.'

'But not enough?'

'To—to sacrifice myself?'

'Do you see it that way? Then let me enlighten you, Farrell. I'm offering you love—I'll wed you with a ring, I'll endow you with all my worldly goods.' His voice grew lower, his expression more serious. 'I'll worship you with my body, Farrell, I'll love and cherish you until the day I die.'

Farrell's heart was thumping, she felt weaker and weaker. She couldn't take her eyes away from his.

She shook her head. 'How—how can you say all those things—now?'

'I can say them because they'll come true. Don't you believe in love at first sight?' he added after a moment.

'I—don't know.'

'I assure you it's a fact of life. And if you suspect I'm simply an opportunist, I'm not. I mean every word I've said. Look, all I ask of you now is that you think about what I've proposed—that you think about me, while I'm away. When I come back, if you're agreeable, I'll have a talk with your father. Then with his permission, I'll take you with me to Quindalup, and we'll discover each other.'

Quindalup? Where was that? But Farrell didn't ask. She merely shook her head again. 'I couldn't possibly—marry you.'

'Forget that bit for a moment, then. And I'll try to forget what you've just said, too,' he said with a slight smile. 'It's not terribly flattering. At all events, in two or three weeks' time you may have second thoughts. You may be ready to go anywhere.'

'No, I shan't,' she argued. 'Why should you say that?'

'I've as good as told you why. You're in for trouble here,' he said positively.

'I'm not in for trouble,' she contradicted him, though she was far from sure of the truth of what she said. 'It—it always takes a little time to adjust to new circumstances. I've only been here for two weeks. Cecile and I will work things out.'

'Have it your own way. But don't forget what I've suggested.'

'I'm hardly likely to,' she said wryly. 'It's not an idea that's presented to a girl every day.'

He smiled back at her, then turned to the waitress who had brought the bill. While he was glancing over it, she studied his face. He was good to look at, she admitted to herself, and she couldn't feel anything like indifferent to him. He had an intelligent forehead, a straight nose, a mouth that had humour lines around it. There were lines around his eyes, too, and his eyes, for her, were his most intriguing feature. But it just didn't make sense that he wanted her to marry him, even though his idea of their getting to know each other had seemed reasonable enough. And he had actually said he'd have a talk with her father!

Farrell simply couldn't imagine her father letting her go off with a man—with *any* man—just like that. But Larry Sandfort wasn't any man. Somehow, she was instinctively aware of that. He just might persuade her father—— What on earth would he say to Daddy? she wondered, and for a moment she wanted to laugh hysterically. But it would never come to that. When he came back—and she didn't have any doubt in her mind that he would come back—she would tell him no again, and that would be the end of it.

She felt a faint and illogical regret that he had to leave tomorrow. He was, at least, more than a little fascinating. She would have liked to get to know him better. But *not* to be pushed into an arrangement so strange as the one he had depicted. By no stretch of the imagination could she picture herself married to him—but then her imagination hadn't had a great deal of exercise in that direction. She'd never met anyone she'd even vaguely thought of marrying. Marriage was a—reality, and there was probably not another girl at the University of Western Australia—or in the whole of Perth—as untutored in even the rudiments of love as Farrell Fitzgerald.

Fleetingly, she wished she hadn't run away from Mark Smith that day on the beach . . .

When she was back in the car with Larry, she more than half expected him to drive to the beach or to some secluded place and make love to her. In fact, she was so nervous and tensed up at the thought of it that it was with a shock she realised they were almost back at the hotel.

He got out of the car to open the door for her, and as she stepped out he took her hand and held it.

'Goodnight, Farrell. Think of me, won't you?'

The pressure of his fingers on hers seemed to communicate something to her. Her arm tingled, and she was aware from this small physical contact that there was something alarmingly real about the whole situation. Perhaps then he might have kissed her, but a group of people came through from the terrace, and Farrell murmured 'Good-night,' withdrew her hand, and hurried away.

CHAPTER TWO

She didn't seem him again. He must have left the hotel early the next morning, but she deliberately refrained from asking her father. Cecile, however, asked about him later in the morning when she sauntered into the reception lobby. Farrell was arranging some long trailing stems of bougainvillea in a big earthenware vase, and her father, on his way through, had stopped to talk to her for a moment.

'Am I interrupting a heart-to-heart?' Cecile asked with a bright smile. She was wearing a green and white flowered dress, and she looked very charming.

Farrell flushed a little at the question, and her father crossed the carpeted floor to put an arm around his wife's bare freckled shoulders.

'You're interrupting nothing, darling. I was on my way to the pool to check the chlorination, and paused to admire Farrell's little floral effort.' He added that, Farrell thought wryly, as if he had to explain why he was talking to his own daughter!

'Very nice,' said Cecile, with a casual glance at the flowers. 'Where's that man Larry Sandfort?' she continued, raising her face to her husband's.

'Checked out this morning. He had to get back to business.'

'Oh? He didn't stay with us for long. Hardly worth a visit. What brought him here, I wonder.'

'I wouldn't know,' he said.

Farrell stooped to pick up a fallen flower. Larry had told her he'd had a little private investigation to carry out—whatever that may have meant. But it was not information she would have passed on even apart from the fact that it seemed more tactful to keep right out of the conversation Cecile was having with her father—even if it was within her hearing. The mention of Larry's name had made her blood leap guiltily, and her fingers shook a little as she painstakingly arranged another long stem in the bowl.

'Well, I'm sorry he's gone. He's certainly a fascinating man,' Cecile remarked. 'Dangerous, too!'

'Oh?' Tony Fitzgerald sounded amused. 'In what way?'

'Darling, if you were a woman you wouldn't have to ask. He's the type who loses no time—one of those charmers who'll start making love to you at the dinner table, five minutes after he's met you. Of course, if you're frightened of passion, you run.'

Farrell almost bit her tongue preventing herself from gasping aloud at this light Cecile was casting on Larry. *Was* he like that? She had had dinner with him—and over it he had asked her to marry him. Cecile—her father—both of them would have a fit if they knew . . . She glanced at her father and saw him raise his eyebrows.

'You make me thankful he's departed. Just how far did he get with you, honey?'

Farrell swallowed hard, but of course he was addressing Cecile, not her.

'No place,' said Cecile. 'He asked me to have a drink with him, and then Farrell decided to join us.'

'Good for Farrell,' Tony Fitzgerald said lightly. 'She must be keeping an eye on my preserves.'

'That I can do without,' Cecile snapped. 'Surely you can trust me, Tony——' She turned on her heel and flounced through the door, and Farrell's heart sank.

'You shouldn't have said that, Daddy,' she said awkwardly. 'I—I wasn't, you know. He—he *asked* me to have a drink——'

'You might do better to keep right out of Cecile's way,' Tony grunted.

'I'm sorry,' Farrell sighed, but her father was already on his way out and didn't hear her.

She finished arranging the flowers, but she had lost heart. It was becoming very plain that Cecile didn't want her here. Even her father was aware of it, with his advice to keep out of her way. But how can you keep out of another woman's way when her husband is your father and you love him and are living with them, even though not in the conventional home setting?

Farrell began to wonder at her wisdom in leaving Perth and flying up here. Aunt Jean had predicted she would regret it, but for a different reason. She positively didn't want to be a teacher or a tutor, or a lecturer like her aunt. Nothing—nothing, she vowed—would make her go back to that eternal studying. She had never been a natural scholar, and since her bout of influenza she had developed an almost pathological aversion to studying. She had known a compulsive need to get away. Her dreams were still haunted by the fear of failing her exams, she still woke sometimes in the dark, heart pounding, wondering if her alarm clock had failed to go off and if she should already have been at her desk doing the early morning study her aunt insisted on. When she was sixteen, she had suffered a minor breakdown. That summer, Aunt Jean had taken her to Tasmania on a holiday that had cost a lot of money. They had made a leisurely tour of a leisurely island, and Farrell had been healed, but her father had never been told about it. 'We don't want to worry him,' her aunt had said. If he had been told, Farrell knew now how concerned he would have been. Her life must have changed then.

Now, she didn't know what she was going to do. One thing was certain—Larry Sandfort's proposition wasn't the way out ...

Later on in the day she escaped over the sandhills to the beach. Lying prone on the sand, the sun—hot already up here north of Capricorn, although it was late winter—lying like a great benevolent hand on her back, she thought of what Cecile had said about Larry. That he was dangerous. That if passion frightened you, you ran. And she, Farrell Fitzgerald, had sat with him at the Lobster Pot, frightened not by his passion—of that she knew nothing—but by the strange, fascinating, exciting proposal he was making her. 'Marry me. You'll never regret it.'

Of course she had been tempted—she admitted it now. Tempted, excited, flattered. But how could she ever, even for an instant, dream of accepting his proposal? She wasn't the sort of girl who could satisfy a passionate man. She didn't even know how to participate in a simple kiss. The purity of her upbringing had left her a babe in the wood—and a frightened one at that.

She didn't see Mark that day, nor on any of several following days, though she spent more and more time on the beach, in an effort to escape from the situation that had developed at the hotel.

She had become anathema to Cecile. Her feeling that something was wrong had developed with alarming rapidity into the knowledge that nothing was going to mend it, that quite certainly she was not going to be able to make her home here, with her father. She was positive now, too, that Cecile had laid down the law to Tony. Half a dozen times she was aware that her father broke off in the middle of an affectionate gesture towards her, when Cecile was there. She was no longer allowed to help in the office, the dining room had become practically forbidden territory, and however tactful Tony tried to be about it, Farrell knew she was being squeezed out by Cecile. Even when she answered the telephone at reception, Cecile took her to task over it.

'I was right there on the terrace, Farrell. I heard the phone ring. My ears are attuned to it. You didn't need to interfere. Why don't you do what you said you wanted to do, the other day, and get on writing your stories or whatever it is you imagine you're qualified to write?'

Farrell's heart hammered. She was torn between anger and frustration, and the inescapable knowledge that she was an intruder. Slowly but surely she was being frozen out, and if she resisted, it was her father who would be hurt. As it was, he wouldn't send her away. That she knew very well.

One morning she woke determined to find herself work somewhere else. It seemed the only thing to do to get herself out of the way, and she was beginning to want that just as much as Cecile. It was terrible—it was as bad as exam days in Perth—to wake in the mornings and face the new day with dread.

She thought of the modern seafood processing plant along the coast, and without telling her father what she intended to do, asked if she could have a loan of his car. 'I'd like to go for a drive, Daddy.' Cecile was there, but even if she hadn't been, Farrell didn't think she would have told her father what she really had in mind. He would be sure to protest.

'Yes, take the car,' Tony said. 'But be careful. I know you have your licence and you probably imagine driving here's a lot safer than in the city. But there are still people on the roads who drive too fast.'

Farrell nodded, aware that Cecile was looking at her curiously.

'You're beginning to be bored, aren't you, Farrell?' She turned to Tony. 'You know, darling, I really think it's time you put your foot down and sent your daughter back to university. Farrell will thank you for it later.'

'What about it, Farrell?' her father said after a moment.

'Would you like to go? Don't feel you'll be lowering the flag if you admit you made a mistake. It's no life for you here.'

Farrell felt tears spring to her eyes because, quite definitely, her father looked hopeful. Two women bickering—bugging him. He must be fed up, she thought. She said lightly, 'I'll think about it, Daddy. I imagined I could help here, but I'm not really any use.'

'No, you're not,' Cecile agreed.

Farrell counted ten and smiled while she did so. 'I'll work something out,' she said finally.

'Then don't take too long about it,' Cecile warned, and she smiled too.

The processing plant was some fifteen minutes' drive along the coast. Farrell took the turn-off and soon reached the plant precincts. Down by the shore she could see the picturesque slightly disreputable-looking trawlers, and some distance from the plant buildings was a group of cabins and caravans where the workers were quartered. She parked her father's car and full of nervous trepidation headed for the plant. From the main building, as she approached, came the sound of machinery overlaid by pop music. A girl in a white cap and wearing a big stiff waterproof apron with her name—Susie—on the bib, came through the door as Farrell drew near, and looked at her questioningly.

'Oh, please,' said Farrell with a bright smile, 'I was wondering if there's any chance of getting work here. Could you tell me who I should see?'

'You'll have to see the boss,' Susie told her. 'He's out just now.' Her friendly eyes wandered over Farrell in her blue jeans and neat navy T-shirt. 'Are you on a working holiday or something? We do take girls for short periods. You wouldn't want a permanent job, would you?'

Farrell swallowed. The noise from the building was

deafening, water gushed everywhere over the cement floor, and there was the sickening smell of prawns. She shook her head bewilderedly. 'I'm—I'm not sure.'

Another girl appeared in the doorway, a pretty Malaysian girl. She grinned and disappeared inside again, and a man emerged with a stack of boxes.

'Would you like to have a look around?' Susie asked amiably. 'We work from six a.m. till seven at night, by the way, and we live across the paddock—the girls in one part, the boys in another. You don't need any experience, you soon catch on.'

Farrell followed her into the noisy room, and saw the girls sorting and packing prawns. There were big tanks where they were washed, and there was a huge modern machine that did the shelling. There was water everywhere, bits of prawn, and that smell!

Farrell suddenly thought she must be mad. She hadn't left Perth to come to this, and she wasn't going to leave the hotel for a job here either—not unless she was absolutely desperate.

Outside once more, she thanked Susie, said somewhat inadequately that she didn't really think she'd like it, and went forlornly back to the car.

Now what did she do? There just weren't any jobs around here ...

That evening on the beach she saw Mark again.

'Hi, Farrell, I hoped I might run into you. I wanted to say goodbye.'

Farrell stared at him blankly. He wore blue jeans and a matching jacket, both of which had once obviously been good but were now faded and shabby. 'What do you mean, goodbye?' she asked, and thought dismally, 'Wouldn't that just be my luck!' Right now, when she needed a friend. 'Where are you going?'

He shrugged. 'I'm not sure. But I've had enough of the

prawning business—it's time to move on.' He threw himself down on the sand, and Farrell sat down near him, hugging her knees, her head lowered, to hide her unhappy face. 'I'll probably go up along the coast. I might find something to do in Port Hedland. Dampier's a company town, and Karratha's partly that way, and I'm not interested in working for any of the mining companies. How are things going with you?'

Farrell didn't answer straight away. An idea had leapt into her mind. Here was a chance to get away! Couldn't she go to Port Hedland with Mark—find herself a job there? She might be able to find some sort of office work. She could type; she had learned touch typing before she started at university. 'It will be invaluable for typing out your essays,' Aunt Jean had said, and though Farrell was hardly expert, she would improve. Anyhow, if there was no office work available she could work in a shop or as a waitress. She would do anything. But not, she reminded herself with an inward grimace, work in a prawn factory!

She looked at the dark-haired, dark-eyed boy sprawling near her on the sand and reflected how different he was from Larry Sandfort. There was nothing dangerous about him! Her heart lifted, and she said excitedly, 'I'd like to come with you, Mark.'

He sat up and stared at her. 'What? Do you mean that?'

He sounded so pleased and so surprised that Farrell laughed aloud. 'Of course I mean it. I want to get away from the hotel, and I can look for a job too.'

'Well, that's great! You're a real surprise packet, Farrell.' His eyes explored her flushed face. 'I didn't think you had it in you. But look, I'm counting on leaving tomorrow.'

'Tomorrow?' she repeated, dismayed.

'Yes, well—I heard something yesterday that makes me suspect someone's located me. Next thing my mother will be trying to rope me in and drag me back to the family fold. So I've got to disappear as fast as I can. Do you see?'

Farrell nodded and hesitated, and then made up her mind. 'All right,' she agreed. 'Tomorrow.' After all, if she was leaving, there was no point in making it a long-drawn-out affair, and if she missed this opportunity she'd probably still be here when Larry Sandfort came back. And she was more than a little scared of what might happen then.

'Good,' Mark approved. 'I don't particularly want to change my plans. No use messing around when your mind's made up anyhow.'

'No,' Farrell agreed. 'Mark, just so I'll know how much I can bring, do you have a car or a motorbike?'

'A car. She's a bit old and beat up, but she's roadworthy. You can bring all you like. I'll pick you up in town if you don't mind—outside Wesfarmers, let's make it, at about ten in the morning.'

'All right.' Farrell forced herself not to think of the difficulties ahead of her. After all, she had faced Aunt Jean with her decision to leave Perth, and in this case Cecile at least was going to be pleased, and even her father would be relieved, she realised a little sadly.

'By the way, Farrell,' Mark said after a short silence, 'you don't plan to tell your parents you and I are teaming up, do you? I'd rather you didn't. I don't want to leave any more of a trail than is absolutely unavoidable.'

'Very well, I shan't tell Daddy,' Farrell consented. 'I'll think of some explanation.' She decided to shelve that problem until she could give her mind to it, and she asked Mark impulsively, 'But Mark, isn't it hard on your parents now knowing where you are? Your mother—she must worry about you.'

'Now don't start on that, Farrell. I know what I'm doing. I'm an adult and I mean to be allowed to act like one. Someone else will have to comfort my mother. I've got to be free—I thought you understood that. I don't want letters designed to tear at my heart strings.'

Farrell was silent. She couldn't help thinking Mark was cruel. She knew she couldn't do that to anyone who loved her. Aunt Jean knew where she was, and she had written to her twice already, although she hadn't yet had a reply. Still, it was up to Mark how he conducted his life. She wondered if travelling to Port Hedland with him would prove to be something in the nature of a crash course in getting to know him, as Larry Sandfort had put it. It could hardly be that, though. Port Hedland wasn't all that far away.

'How long will it take us to get to Port Hedland, Mark?' she asked idly, trickling a handful of sand through her fingers and watching it run out.

'Your guess is as good as mine. It depends what turns up on the way there and how fast we travel. I reckon it's only about six or seven hundred kilometres, but we mightn't even get there, you know. My plans are pretty flexible ... Do you still want to come?'

'Yes,' Farrell said slowly. He hadn't asked exactly why she wanted to come, and just now she didn't feel like telling him about the rather undignified situation that prevailed between herself and her stepmother. Perhaps later she might mention it. What hurt, of course, was the estrangement between herself and her father, and that, she suspected, Mark would not want to hear about and would not understand.

Still thinking of his mother, she asked him, 'Do you have any brothers and sisters, Mark?'

'One sister, Helen, older than I am. She lives in Perth, and she writes home, and she comes back for holidays. So quit feeling sorry for my mother, because that's what you're doing, isn't it?'

'I suppose so. Well, I'd better go home and pack my bags and—and explain things, somehow, to my father.'

'Do that. I'll see you in the morning.'

They parted and Farrell went back to the hotel rather slowly. What on earth *was* she going to tell her father?

Lies, obviously. She could hardly tell him she was going to Port Hedland with a boy whose identity she refused to divulge. Or with a boy at all, if it came to that. Her father wouldn't approve in any case, not even if Mark came to the hotel and spoke to him about it. That was what Larry Sandfort had said he'd do—— 'With your father's permission, I'll take you to Quindalup.' Now, she would never find out where Quindalup was.

In her room, she packed her things—all of them. She had left most of her warm clothes in Perth, so she didn't have a great deal. As she packed she tried to think what she would tell her father. She hated having to lie, but there seemed to be no alternative, and when at last she wandered out in search of him, she had decided that she would say—that she was going to Port Hedland to find work, and that she was getting a lift with some girls she'd met in the town. That should pass as long as he didn't grill her.

She found him occupied, and it was not until dinner time—it was not a smorgasbord that night—that she managed to talk to him at all, and then she had to do so in Cecile's presence.

She had joined her father and stepmother in one of the small rooms off the main dining room where they could have their meal privately, but where Tony would be available if he were wanted. Somehow, the atmosphere was strained, and conversation was almost non-existent. Farrell wondered unhappily if it was because she was there, if they wanted to be alone, if her constant presence was beginning to disturb even her father. It seemed a good thing she was going.

'Do you know what I did today?' she asked with a determined effort at bright casualness as she tried to get up some interest in the main course.

'No. What was that?' her father asked, turning his head to look at her. Cecile said nothing, but a quick glance showed Farrell that her expression meant, 'Who cares what you did?'

'Well, I was talking to some girls—when I went out for that drive, you know,' Farrell elaborated. 'They've—they've been working at the prawn factory, but they've decided to move on to Port Hedland to look for work there. I—I thought I might go with them and find a job myself,' she concluded, rather amazed at her inventiveness.

Now she had Cecile's interested attention, but Tony frowned. 'Now what sort of a job would you get in Port Hedland, Farrell?' he asked wearily. 'You don't have any training. Frankly, if you feel like a move, I think the sensible thing would be to go back to your aunt in Perth and get on with your university course. With a degree, you'll have some chance of picking and choosing where you go.'

'Daddy, no,' Farrell said determinedly. 'I know you're disappointed in me, but I'd really be terribly unhappy if—if you made me go back to that.'

'I shan't *make* you do anything, Farrell,' Tony said. 'God forbid! You're an adult——'

'Who doesn't act like one,' Cecile put in sharply. 'If you want my opinion, Tony, an immature girl of nineteen's not too old to be told what to do and to be made to do it. However, if Farrell's going to be pig-headed let her go to Port Hedland. She'll get work if she has to—she's always insisting she'll do room-cleaning or kitchen work here if it's required of her.'

'I'm not having my daughter do that kind of work—not here, and certainly not anywhere else,' Tony retorted, glaring at his wife. 'If that's the alternative to her staying here with us, then she can stay here.'

It sounded, Farrell thought, as if they'd already argued about her, and perhaps they had. It would account for the strained silence that had existed before she had opened this discussion. She said quickly, 'Daddy, don't *worry*—don't get upset. I can do typing, you know, and I'll look for *office* work. Mar—Margaret says I could get something in that line in Port Hedland.'

'You might and you might not,' he said shortly. 'Who are these girls, anyhow? Not local girls——'

Farrell coloured slightly and hoped she didn't look as guilty as she felt. She wished too that Cecile would stop staring at her, as if she were suspicious in some way. 'They're from—from Bunbury,' she improvised. 'They're on a working holiday in the Pilbara. And they're leaving tomorrow,' she finished, feeling she might as well get it over.

'Tomorrow?' her father exclaimed explosively. 'Do you mean you plan to leave *tomorrow*?'

'*Tony*,' Cecile interrupted, 'don't get apoplectic about it. What's the difference if Farrell goes tomorrow or the day after, or in the middle of next week? If she's made up her mind she's tired of idling her time away, she might as well go when she has the opportunity.'

Tony looked at Farrell broodingly. 'Well, I suppose I must allow you to go. But if you don't get work, then don't drift into something that's not good enough for you, no matter what these other girls are doing. I'd certainly never allow *you* to work in the prawn factory. I really wish you'd think about it and go back to university.'

'I've told you she's not going to do that,' Cecile said impatiently. 'You might as well accept it.'

Farrell felt like bursting into tears. So they *had* been discussing her, arguing about her. Cecile had been pressing that something be done about her, and Tony had probably put it that she'd go back to Perth in her own good time. Larry Sandfort had certainly been right in predicting she was in for trouble, and the sooner she got away the better. She didn't want to be left so desperate that she might even take up *his* offer!

She said with an effort at calmness, hoping they didn't notice the quaver in her voice, 'I'm sorry about university, Daddy. I suppose you must think I'm being unreasonable, but I just *can't* go back to that life.'

'And if you want to be a writer,' Cecile said, smiling maliciously, 'you must have experience of the world, of course.'

'What the hell does that mean?' Tony asked angrily. 'And who says Farrell wants to be a writer?'

'She told Larry Sandfort so the other day,' Cecile said sweetly. 'You don't know all Farrell's secrets by any means, Tony, any more than I do.'

Farrell pushed her chair back and stood up. 'I—I wish you wouldn't quarrel about me.' She was scarcely able to hold back her tears. 'Can't we just leave it that I'll go to Port Hedland and try to find a—a respectable job? If I can't, I'll—I'll go back to Perth and find work there.'

Her father she could see she was making an effort to control himself.

'Very well, Farrell. But you're to keep in touch with me, do you hear? I'll give you a month to settle into something decent and steady. If by the end of that time nothing's eventuated, you'll come back here and we'll talk again. And I'll be the one to decide what's to be done about your future.'

'All right, Daddy,' said Farrell, her voice trembling. Already she could see herself being packed off back to Perth to live with Aunt Jean, and then the pressure would be on again for her to resume her studies. She thought about Mark and for the first time began to understand why he had gone into smoke. Parents did resist seeing you as an adult, they did want to push you about—even if it was because they loved you.

She developed a sick headache before she went to bed that night, and woke in the morning wishing she could simply stay in bed for the day, as she usually did on these occasions. If she could have got in touch with Mark, she'd have asked him to delay his departure till tomorrow, when she'd be feeling better. He would be sure to understand. But under the circumstances, there was nothing to do but get up, take some aspirin, and make the best of a miserable situation.

She gave breakfast a miss, settling for two cups of instant coffee that she prepared in her room, and then sought out her father to say goodbye. She thought he looked tired —hag-ridden, maybe! But he was affectionate and more like himself, and she hoped he and Cecile had made up their quarrel. She hated the thought of being the cause of a rift between them.

Tony gave her some notes and said, 'This will tide you over for a while, Farrell. Open a bank account for yourself in Port Hedland with a couple of dollars, then let me have the number and I'll at least be able to see you're not short of cash. It's a pity you don't feel able to go back to your aunt in Perth, but the most important thing is for you to be happy. And you haven't been altogether happy here, have you?'

Farrell shook her head, blinking back tears and forcing a smile. 'I'm too old to fit into a family, I suppose,' she said wryly. Neither of them mentioned Cecil—it was better that way—but at least her stepmother made an effort too and said goodbye to Farrell very pleasantly, and even wished her luck.

Well, *she* had what she wanted, Farrell thought sardonically. To her relief, Cecile didn't go so far as to offer to drive her into the small town to meet her girl friends, and there were no protests when Farrell rang for a taxi.

She was waiting outside Wesfarmers with her luggage a little before ten, but it was almost a quarter of an hour before Mark arrived.

'You look crook, Farrell,' was his first remark as he got out to deal with her bags.

Farrell gave him a watery smile. 'I *feel* crook,' she agreed. 'But it's nothing—I'll be fine tomorrow.'

He nodded understandingly. 'I'd thought of pushing it a bit and trying to make Port Hedland tonight, but it's not good going, so we'll take it easy. Do it in two stages. Okay?'

'That suits me perfectly, Mark,' she said gratefully, climbing into the front seat.

A few moments later they were on their way, and in no time the tiny town was left behind and they were heading north-west. Mark didn't ask what she had told her father or what the family reaction had been, and for this she was grateful. She didn't want to go over the scene that had taken place at dinner last night, but preferred to keep at the front of her mind the fact that her father had been loving and generous this morning and that Cecile had been pleasant too. Leaning back in the seat she thought presently, without meaning to, of Larry Sandfort. What would he think—what would he do—when he came back and found her gone? Well, he could hardly be surprised. That proposal of his had been just so way out it wasn't true. No sane reasonable girl would have taken it up, unless she had fallen in love with him at first sight, and though Farrell had certainly been affected by his magnetic personality, she hadn't done that. She only hoped he wouldn't take it into his head to follow her to Port Hedland—he would have to be really keen to do that!

Well, she followed up that thought, wouldn't he have to be really keen to have suggested to her what he had suggested? Keen to get himself a wife, that was—not keen on her. She couldn't imagine a man like him falling in love with anyone at first sight.

She laughed aloud and Mark turned his head.

'What's funny?'

'Nothing,' she said weakly. 'Just my silly thoughts.'

He let it pass. Farrell, who didn't feel like talking, closed her eyes. She heard Cecile's voice saying, 'You don't know all Farrell's secrets by any means.' No one knew all Farrell's secrets. Probably Mark had secrets too. She wondered how much of their private, personal lives and problems they would confide in each other today and tomorrow. And whether they would see much of each other after they reached Port Hedland. Perhaps she would tell Mark about Larry Sandfort. She didn't think so.

Mark drove fast on the narrow bitumen road, then slowed down perforce when he took to the fifty or so kilometres of gravel that linked up with the North-West Coastal Highway. Farrell relaxed as much as she was able, though the bumpy road didn't really help. Mark didn't expect her to make conversation and she put on her sun-glasses and looked out mindlessly at the red, red sandhill country they were driving through. It was very beautiful to the eye, the pure unblemished red of the sands blurred by the green and straw of spinifex clumps. The road was rose pink, banked up at the sides where the grader had been through. They were passing through sheep stations, though not a single dwelling was to be seen, and only sheep grazing occasionally in the scrub indicated that man had settled here at all. Farrell was reminded that Mark's father owned a sheep station, but she didn't stir herself to ask him about him, as she leaned back musing on the vastness and the emptiness of the state where it was more usual to see an emu or a kangaroo than a human being.

They stopped for lunch some way up the bitumen at one of the roadhouses that were often the only sign of civilisation up here in a couple of hundred kilometres. There, one could buy petrol, a few basic provisions, get a meal and a drink and perhaps a bed for the night. Farrell slept like a log that night at another such roadhouse this side of Dampier.

She felt better when she woke in the morning, and she was as eager as Mark to reach Port Hedland and start looking for work. They skimmed over the empty highway, pausing to take a look at Dampier where the salt glistened like snow in the bay, for the tide was out, and they saw the great iron ore trucks that were being unloaded before they went back along the company railway line to Mount Tom Price. They drove past Karratha and Roebourne and on through the spinifex country that spread all across the north of the million-square-mile state. It was monotonous, but pretty, highlighted as it was by the pink and mauve ranges that floated against the southern horizon.

Farrell began to feel she was a long way from home—a long way from anybody, totally dependent on Mark.

'We'll put up at a motel in Port Hedland tonight,' Mark decided as they came off a long gravel stretch that had begun at Roebourne and ended at the Yule River—one of the many rivers of the north that would flood when the rains came but were dry for most of the year.

'Do you know Port Hedland, Mark?' Farrell asked.

He shook his head. 'Never been there in my life. A couple of guys were saying that the cheapest way to accommodate yourself is to rent a caravan in the caravan park. Lots of people do it—live there more or less permanently. Sounds just the shot for us, but it will depend on the work situation, of course. If we don't find anything, we'll move on.'

He stopped talking as a flock of galahs rose in a flurry of pink and silver from the middle of the road, and Farrell glanced at him thoughtfully. He said 'we' and 'us' so naturally. She wasn't at all sure she wanted to share a caravan with him, however, and she was a little surprised he seemed to take it for granted they were going to stick

together. Did she *want* to stick with Mark? She didn't
really know. She didn't want to be on her own, of course,
and Mark was pleasant, easy to get on with, but——

Farrell gave up and rather lazily shelved her thoughts.
She would deal with all that when she had to ...

It was just on dark when they reached Port Hedland.
Farrell was tired, and somehow she was disappointed. The
town didn't attract her, she didn't have a feeling of welcome—and yet she had heard guests at her father's hotel
speak glowingly of the place, or the easygoing camaraderie
there. Mark found the motel and she waited wearily in the
car while he went to see if they could book in. When he
came back he told her, 'Only one vacancy—a room with
twin beds. Is that all right with you? It's cheaper that way
anyhow—twenty-eight dollars for a double, twenty-two
each for single rooms.'

Farrell bit her lip. It would be just for one night, of
course, but—

'Well?' Mark insisted. 'Do we take it or don't we? It's
up to you—only remember accommodation's pretty hard to
come by here. D'you want me to ask to use the phone and
see if I can get reservations somewhere else? I'll give it a
go—'

'Oh, don't bother, Mark—it's all right. Tomorrow——'

'Tomorrow we'll make an early start and look for work,'
Mark said. He grinned at her happily and got into the car.
He drove to the parking area, then got their luggage out.

'Don't you have to go back to the office and book in?'
Farrell wanted to know.

'I've already done that,' he said off-handedly. 'I knew
you wouldn't have any objections, Farrell.'

'But I might have had,' Farrell thought, and wondered if
she had made a bad mistake.

Their room was a big one with two beds, a refrigerator,
facilities for making tea or coffee, a modern shower room

and toilet. And it was air-conditioned. When Mark had brought the luggage in he went into the bathroom, then emerged and told Farrell, 'I'm going along to the bar for a drink. I'll see if I can pick up any info about the work situation. I'll see you in the dining room in about half an hour.'

'All right,' Farrell agreed.

When he had gone, she unpacked her toilet things and night attire. Then she showered, and got into a creamy silky dress, patterned with clusters of tiny red and black flowers. Mark was very tactful about getting out of her way, but she didn't feel very happy about sharing a room, even though she was somehow convinced that she was perfectly safe with him. She was pretty sure he would have signed the register as Mr and Mrs Smith, but after all, what did it matter?—except her father would have a fit if he knew. So he just wouldn't know. Anyhow, she could look after herself, she wasn't a fool.

The dining room was attractive and the food was expensive, but it was good. They both chose seafood, and followed up with fruit salad and cream.

'What did you find out about work?' Farrell asked over the coffee.

'Not much. But it doesn't sound too hopeful. I get the feeling I wouldn't like to work here, anyway.'

Farrell frowned. 'It may be just a matter of getting acclimatised. I suppose there's an employment agency—or we could look in the local paper,' she added thoughtfully.

'Sure, we'll do all of that—we'll give it a go.'

He smiled at her, and she smiled back. Everything was going to be all right, she was sure of it.

CHAPTER THREE

AFTER three days, neither of them had found work. Farrell's lack of qualifications didn't help, and Mark didn't seem easy to please—or so Farrell gathered.

Meanwhile, at fourteen dollars a day each, plus meals, Farrell's money at least was running out too fast for her liking, and she didn't want to bother her father for more in too much of a hurry.

'I reckon we'll move on,' Mark said that night. They were still at the motel, and Farrell had gone to bed. Mark, who had been talking to someone in the lounge, had come in ten minutes ago. He always gave Farrell plenty of time to get herself ready for bed before he came in, and always, as he had tonight, he undressed in the bathroom. She was grateful to him for this, for it made the situation acceptable and gave her a feeling of confidence in him. Now, in briefs—he didn't wear pyjamas—and with a towel around his neck, he stood at the mirror combing his longish dark hair which he washed every night. Though his body was slim, he had good arm and shoulder muscles, but his chest, which the towel partly covered, was marred by some ugly scars. Farrell had never seen those scars till they had come to Port Hedland, for she and Mark had never swum or sunbathed together and whenever she had met him on the beach he had been wearing a shirt. She had uttered a little half-smothered exclamation of shock when first she saw him stripped to the waist.

'Oh, Mark, whatever happened?'

He had grimaced, reached for his towel and slung it round his neck. 'Is that better? It's nothing anyhow—just a few scars that are fading. I was in an accident a year or so ago. Forget it.'

Aware that he didn't want to talk about it, she asked no more questions and now she was used to the sight of him, and lying on her back, her hands behind her neck, she watched him absentmindedly.

'Well,' he said, turning towards her and coming to sit on the side of her bed, 'what do you think?'

'About moving on? We haven't given it much of a try yet really, have we? Something could turn up tomorrow——'

'Could, but I bet it won't. I'm not all keen on this town anyhow—or on staying too long in this motel.'

Farrell agreed with that!

'I'll pay my half of the bill, of course,' she said quickly. 'And didn't you say something about caravans for hire?'

'Sure I did, and I've enquired, but there's none available right now.' He stood up, hands on his narrow hips, looking down at her. 'Let's move down the Great Northern, Farrell, this is too much like the big smoke. We might find something in one of those little places—Marble Bar or'—he shrugged—'well, I don't know—somewhere. We can always come back if we want to. What about it? Are you coming or staying?'

Farrel hesitated. For an instant she had a longing to go back to her father's hotel—to safety, she supposed. But that would be admitting defeat and she would be back with her dilemma. On the other hand, the thought of staying on here on her own was far from attractive.

'I'm coming, Mark,' she said finally.

'Beaut!' He grinned, then stooped and kissed her quickly. 'I'm getting used to having you around, Farrell. In fact, I'm beginning to like it. What about you?'

Farrell swallowed nervously. She didn't know what to say. In fact, she wasn't altogether sure what he was asking her. She didn't want to give him the idea she had fallen in love with him, but neither did she want him to feel she didn't appreciate his kindness and consideration. Because he *had* been kind and considerate, and she had no complaints. The one thing that made her uneasy was that he always kissed her goodnight, though never in a demanding way or even in a way that taught her anything about the art of kissing. But she was not so simple that she didn't know this state of affairs wasn't going to last, and now as Mark leaned over her again, a hand on the pillow at either side of her head, she moved uneasily.

'Well,' he repeated, his voice softening, 'do you like it too, Farrell?'

There was a look in his dark eyes that said he was going to kiss her again—and in a rather different way if she made the right response, and she felt herself stiffen immediately.

'Yes, but——' she faltered, and pushed herself further down under the bedclothes.

'Okay, don't get worked up, I know how to behave myself. I can wait,' he said. Then to her relief he said goodnight and got into his own bed.

Farrell didn't fall asleep for some time. She was beginning to wonder what she had got herself into. Well, she hadn't got herself into anything yet. She had said she would go with Mark, and she supposed she would, but there would be no more sharing rooms. At least once they moved out of Port Hedland she could put an end to *that*. And then if they were going to fall in love with each other they could do so in a more conventional way, though Farrell didn't really feel she was ready to fall in love with *anyone* yet ...

They left Port Hedland rather late the following morning, mainly because Farrell had insisted on writing a letter to her father. In it, she told him merely that she hadn't found work yet, but that her money was holding out. She didn't— *couldn't*—bring herself to mention the fictitious girls she was supposed to have travelled with, and feeling guilty and ashamed, she didn't tell him either that she was moving on. If Larry Sandfort turned up looking for her, her father would tell him she had gone to Port Hedland and that would be that. He might look, but he wouldn't find her, and that would be a good thing. Not that she disliked him, on the contrary, he was very impressive, very personable, and there was something about him that intrigued her, and if she sat down and thought about it, she felt more and more amazed that a man like that should have asked her to marry him. But of course she couldn't—she'd be frightened out of her senses.

The highway they travelled on that day was a gravel road, and there was nothing on it that could really be called a town until Meekatharra, some nine hundred kilometres distant. About half way to Perth, in fact. This information was given to Mark at the garage where he filled up with petrol before they went on their way, and it flashed through Farrell's mind that it was hardly likely either she or Mark would find work between here and Meekatharra. She hadn't fully realised what a vast and empty state Western Australia was, and she reflected that without doubt they would be back in Port Hedland before long. So her father need never know——

They travelled a long way that day, over the spinifex-clad tableland and into the Chichester Ranges, then across a desolate granite plain that looked as if it could never support human life. Farrell began to understand why it was that three-quarters of the state's population lived in Perth! It was a relief to find somewhere they could stop for the night—one of the little roadhouses that provided petrol and a few simple amenities. Despite Farrell's determination to have a room to herself, it seemed there was nothing she could do about it this time, and defeatedly she preceded Mark into a room that was no more than adequate.

There was a primitive bathroom across the yard, and

Farrell showered first, and dressed while Mark took his turn. It had been a tiring day, but now she felt slightly refreshed. Darkness had fallen and the air was cooling when they went to the small restaurant attached to the garage, and had a very plain meal. After that, there was nothing to do—spinifex and dark ironstone flats all around, not a light showing anywhere in the night beyond those at the little roadside stop. When they came out of the restaurant, Mark started up a conversation with the proprietor, and Farrell yawned.

'Your wife looks tired,' the man commented, and she flushed, and said quickly, 'I think I'll go to bed.' She smiled a goodnight, and went away thankfully.

She got herself to bed quickly, hoping Mark would take his time and she would be sound asleep when he came. She had left the reading lamp on—there was only one, it gave a very poor light and it was by the other bed, and she turned her face to the wall and closed her eyes determinedly.

It was only a short time after, and she was still wide awake when she heard him come in. She lay still, pretending to be asleep, and listening to the small sounds he made as he moved about getting ready for bed.

'Farrell?'

She said nothing, but her heart thudded.

'Farrell,' he repeated. And now his voice was close to her ear, and she felt the movement of the mattress as he sat down on her bed. It was no use pretending to be asleep now, and she turned over and looked at him. He was naked to the waist and the scars showed livid on his chest. He slid his arm beneath her neck and lowered his mouth to hers. Farrell struggled to escape from him, but she was trapped between the wall and his insistent weight, and it was seconds before she managed to wrench her mouth away from his.

'Mark—*don't*——'

'Oh, come on, Farrell,' he murmured. He stroked her cheek with his fingers and brushed his lips across her eyelids, but the weight of his body didn't lift. 'Don't look so scared. I won't do anything you don't want. I'm not that stupid——'

He kissed her again and she felt panic rising in her. She was beginning to feel sick, and when she felt his hand come under the bedclothes and his fingers begin to unfasten her pyjama-top buttons she twisted her head violently aside and shocked even herself by screaming.

Instantly his hand was hard over her mouth.

'For God's sake, shut up! I'm not going to do anything to you——'

'Let me go,' Farrell muttered against his hand. She made frantic efforts to push him away from her. 'Go away—go *away*, do you hear?'

He thumped her arm. 'Stop shoving—I've got the message,' he said through his teeth. 'What's wrong with you, anyhow? You asked could you come with me—what do you think I took that to mean? Not that you wanted a nursemaid—I've looked after you, haven't I? And now just because I start cuddling you, you scream your head off, like I'm some kind of monster.' He paused and glared at her angrily. 'What's *wrong* with you, Farrell?'

'Nothing,' she gulped, and flung her arm across her eyes. 'Just—leave me alone—don't touch me——'

She felt him get up from the bed and then heard the sounds of the light being switched off and the bed creaking as he got into it.

Farrell lay on her back trying not to cry. Now Mark would think she was a prig and a cold frog too—and perhaps she was. She hadn't needed to scream. But oh, how naïve and stupid she had been in every way! Of course Mark took it for granted she would accept his kisses! Any

normal girl would. And she didn't believe for a moment he
had intended to do more than——

'Mark,' she whispered huskily into the darkness.

'What?' His voice was hard, unfriendly.

'I'm—sorry. It was just——'

'Just *what*?' he bit out. 'If you dislike me all that much
you shouldn't have come along. A kiss or two isn't going to
hurt you, is it?'

'No, but—I'm sorry. I don't know why I screamed.
And—and I do like you, Mark——'

She heard him laugh without amusement. 'I don't like
your way of showing it, then. All I did was kiss you. Have
you been brought up to think sex is wrong or something,
and that nice girls don't cuddle?'

Farrell clenched her fists under the bedclothes. Maybe
she had been brought up that way. Maybe that was the
whole trouble. She could hear Aunt Jean's voice saying
coolly, 'Sex is just an ugly reminder that man is part of the
animal world.' She drew a deep breath.

'I—I think you'd better take me back to Port Hedland
tomorrow, Mark.'

'Do you? Well, I'm not going to Port Hedland, Farrell.
I'm going on to Meekatharra. You can't have everything
your own way.'

'I know,' she said dejectedly. 'But it's no use our going
on together.'

'It isn't, if that's the way you feel,' he agreed.

When she woke in the morning, his bed was empty, and
she got up and dressed hastily, thinking he had probably
gone over to the bathroom. She knew she would have to go
on to Meekatharra with Mark. Under the circumstances she
could hardly expect him to take her all the way back to Port
Hedland, and she had had a cheek to ask it of him. She only
hoped that relations between them wouldn't be too strained.

Her blood froze at the memory of last night, and at her

hysterical reaction to his touch. She *liked* Mark, after all. The only thing she couldn't understand about him was his ability to leave his mother to worry about his whereabouts. That was, if not cruel, at least unkind.

It was not till she went to the rather spotty mirror to fix her hair that she saw a folded sheet of paper lying on the dressing table with her name on it. She opened it with fingers that shook.

'Dear Farrell,' she read, 'I've paid the bill and am going on to Meekatharra. If you hang around you're sure to get a lift back to Port Hedland, then it's up to you what you do. Maybe you'd better go back home to your parents. Mark.'

Farrell tore the page up slowly and stared out through the window at the bare red yard beyond which was nothing. So she was on her own. She tried not to think it had been mean of Mark to desert her like this, but it *had* been mean. There was no railway up here in this empty land, apart from a few iron ore company-owned lines that didn't transport passengers anyhow. There were no buses, and she had no idea how far she would have to go to find a settlement where there was an air service. It was all very well for Mark to say she would get a lift—the highway was so deserted she might have to wait for days, unless she was prepared to take a chance and go with the first person who came along.

She used the bathroom, then went across to the restaurant and breakfasted on tea and toast. She didn't feel hungry, and she hated the curious glances of the rather sleazy girl who waited on the table. It required an immense effort after she had packed her bags to go to the proprietor and tell him brightly, 'I'm looking for a lift to Port Hedland. Would you—er—keep an eye out for me?'

He looked her over curiously, but to her relief he didn't ask what had happened that she was parting from her 'husband'. He probably hadn't been fooled by that fiction, anyhow, she realised, with a feeling of shame that made her cheeks hot.

'Yair—I'll give a yell if anyone's going that way,' he said obligingly enough.

Farrell put in a restless and miserable day. It wasn't till early afternoon that anyone came to the roadhouse at all. A couple of cars had gone by, but it was completely beyond Farrell to stand beside the road and try to thumb a lift. Then a truck driver stopped for petrol, and after a moment she saw him stroll over to the restaurant. The roadhouse proprietor jerked his head in Farrell's direction, and though he didn't give her a yell, she understood that here was her chance of a lift. She waited outside under the cloudless sky for the truck driver to appear again. She hadn't had any lunch, and didn't want any—food would have choked her.

Presently the truck driver emerged and came over to where she was waiting. He looked her over pretty thoroughly, then asked her with a grin, 'You the girl who's looking for a lift to Port Hedland? Here, give us your bags and hop in.'

Farrell smiled uncertainly and did so. He looked all right, she told herself, determinedly cheerful. He was big and husky and he wore khaki shorts and a short-sleeved shirt, open at the neck and showing a bush of hair.

As they started off, he offered her cigarettes, which she refused with a smile. He lit one up for himself and told her, 'Name's George. You can call me that or anything else that turns you on.'

'My name's—Farrell!' she responded after an instant, because it was expected of her.

He cocked his rather bushy eyebrows. 'Miss? You're too young for a missus. What's your first name?'

Farrell swallowed. 'Jean,' she said after a moment. It seemed easier than explaining that Farrell was her first name, and it didn't matter much in any case.

After an hour or so of driving, George's hand began to wander to Farrell's thigh. She edged away towards the window, but he had no hesitation in reaching out and pulling her back.

'Aw, come on, Jeanie—I'm doing you a favour, remember. You can be a little bit friendly, can't you?'

Farrell had no idea how to handle the situation. She couldn't insist he should either let her alone or allow her to get out of the truck—that would be asking for trouble. She wished she were one of those girls who could make some smartly confident and perhaps amusing retort that would put George in his place yet maintain a good relationship. But she wasn't, and all she could do was sit where she was with that great hot hairy paw resting on her thigh, and pray that George would expect nothing more in the way of—friendliness.

Her heart gave a leap of fright when not much later he swung the truck off the highway on to a side road. There was a signpost, but Farrell had seen it too late to read what it said, and but for the fact that the road was, astonishingly, bitumen, she'd have thought they were heading for one of the sheep properties.

'Where are we going?' she asked uneasily, knowing at least that this was not the way to Port Hedland.

'Nowhere—or as good as. To Ansell. Ever heard of it?'

Yes, Farrell had heard of the iron ore mine at Mount Ansell, but she knew no more about it than she did about Newman or Tom Price or Paraburdoo. She had never been to any of the inland mining towns.

'It's a company town, isn't it?' she asked.

'That's right, Jeanie. Completely owned by Ansell-Sandfort Mining. I've got an order to drop off there. You'll be able to stretch your legs.'

Farrell had given a start. Ansell-Sandfort! That must be the company Larry Sandfort was connected with. She said vaguely, 'I'll be glad to stretch my legs.'

George turned his head and grinned at her. 'We won't be in Port Hedland till after dark, you know.'

'I—I realise that.' Her glance went instinctively to the huge hairy forearms revealed by the short-sleeved shirt, and she shuddered inwardly at the thought of travelling at night with this man. As the truck rolled rapidly along the smooth bitumen road, a jumble of ideas chased each other through her mind. Couldn't she look for Larry Sandfort in Ansell— ask his help? But would he be there, or was he still in Perth at the mining offices? He might even be on his way to the Coral Reef Hotel! In any event, she made up her mind quite definitely she was going no further with George. But she thought she'd keep quiet about it. She'd wait till he'd dropped off his order and sneak her bags out of the truck and disappear. Leave a note so he wouldn't go looking for her. Yes, that was what she would do. She could stay over-night at the hotel—there was bound to be one—and then—— At that moment they passed a turn-off signposted Aerodrome, and her heart lifted. She thought in relief, 'I'll be able to take a plane to Port Hedland.'

A few minutes later the town of Ansell appeared. It was as unexpected as an oasis, isolated here in the middle of nowhere on the flat red spinifex plain, ringed about with bare ranges, their long ridges crowned with square-cut red rocks that looked like the crumbling walls of ancient fort-resses, as they glowed in the afternoon sun.

'It's incredible!' she exclaimed, as they drove down a street edged with green lawns, spreading out from modern homes shaded by big trees—homes with air-conditioning plants in evidence, with solar heating cylinders on their roofs. Sprinklers spun and glittered, greenery flourished, bright tropical flowers were everywhere, poincianas spread their feathery branches. 'It's all so green!'

'Yair. It's had mobs of money poured into it,' George

said laconically, negotiating a corner. 'No one'll stay out here long unless the living conditions are extra good. It's too isolated—and the climate's a cow. Even with all this'—he waved a large hand as they passed a sports centre complete with Olympic-type swimming pool—'labour turnover's somewhere around forty-five per cent.' He swung the wheel again and drove into the parking lot in front of a modern arcaded shopping complex. 'This is where I do my stuff.'

He got out and slammed the door shut. 'You'll find a Ladies in the park, Jeanie. Get yourself a can of Coke if you want it—we'll leave in twenty minutes or so.'

Farrell nodded. She waited nervously until he had opened the back of the truck before she slipped out of her seat and crossed the road to the park. There she found a seat out of sight, ripped a page from the small diary in her handbag, and scribbled 'Thanks' on it. It seemed pointless to write any more—he'd get the idea—and anyhow she didn't have any definite plans other than to avoid having to travel on with him and probably fight him off when it was dark, or even before that.

After a few minutes she hurried back to the truck, put her note and a couple of dollars on the front seat, dragged her suitcases on to the ground and looked about her. A young woman pushing a stroller with an infant in it looked rather curiously, and Farrell asked her on impulse, 'Could you tell me where the—hotel is, please?'

'The Ansell you'd want,' the woman said pleasantly. She pointed along the street. 'You see where the bank is—the Commonwealth? Turn the corner there and it's a little way along on your left.'

'Thank you,' Farrell breathed. She picked up her bags and walked quickly along the footpath towards the bank. It struck her as she hurried along that she needn't go back to Port Hedland, she could find work here if, as George had said, people were quitting their jobs so often. There absolutely must be *something* she could do. Suddenly she felt a lot more cheerful. She didn't really want to return to Port Hedland, nor did she want to go back to her father's hotel and have decisions made about her future. She knew only too well she would be packed off back to Aunt Jean. And the month her father had granted her had hardly begun. Perhaps it was a good thing after all that Mark had walked out on her. She really couldn't blame him for doing so either—though that was something she didn't particularly want to think about just now.

By the time she reached the Ansell Hotel—only it was the Ansell Motel, she noticed, she was feeling more than slightly sick. Inside, she set her suitcases down and put a hand on her forehead, feeling the perspiration of nausea on it. What on earth was the matter with her? It took her a minute to remember that she hadn't eaten anything all day except for a slice of toast at breakfast time. She found her way to the reception desk and asked if she could have a room, and when she had signed the register, she asked the woman who looked friendly, 'Could you tell me if it would be possible to find work in Ansell? I'm looking for something—well, for anything, really.'

While she was speaking a door behind the desk opened and a man appeared and stood listening. As she finished speaking he came forward.

'Excuse me, Alice'—this was to the receptionist. 'Now, Miss—er—Fitzgerald,' he continued with a quick glance at her signature, 'my name's Forbes. I'm the manager here. In answer to your question, this is a company-owned town, and no matter what kind of work you're looking for, all appointments are made through the offices in Perth.'

Farrell was slightly taken aback. 'All? Surely—surely *waitresses* aren't appointed in Perth!' she exclaimed.

He smiled slightly. 'Oh dear me, yes—if necessary, the

company would have applicants screened by a Perth agency. But as a general rule, wives of male employees here are recruited as waitresses and bar staff. The majority of couples here are out to make good money, you know. They're not here for the climate or the social life. You wouldn't want to do that kind of work anyhow,' he added smoothly.

'Why not?' Farrell said coolly. 'I've had some—some hotel experience,' she added, for that was certainly true in a limited way.

'*Not* in a company town,' he said flatly. 'Quite frankly, Miss Fitzgerald, I wouldn't advise you to seek work in Ansell at all. You don't look the type who could cope with it.'

'If you mean the climate,' Farrell countered, tossing back her fair curls and aware that hunger and weariness probably made her look far from robust, 'that wouldn't worry me. I'm healthy enough—'

'I'm not talking about the climate. There's a shortage of women here, and you can work out for yourself what that means.'

Farrell, in her present condition, couldn't. She could hardly think straight at all, and she heard herself say stiffly, 'Would mentioning Larry Sandfort's name make any difference? I *need* a job and I'm—I'm a friend of his.'

The manager looked sceptical. 'Mentioning his name wouldn't help one little bit, dear. And for your information, he left this morning for the coast in his plane, so you won't be able to call on him to back you up. I'm afraid I can't help you at all.'

Farrell gave in and moved away thoughtfully. So Larry had left for the coast—to look for her? She trembled a little at the thought.

She carried her luggage through to where a wide sloping roof shaded a walk around a paved court. A little gateway under a swathe of yellow-flowered vines led to the motel units. Farrell's was number twenty-four. She unlocked the door and stepped into a cool whitewashed room with a slanting ceiling supported by heavy black beams. There were twin beds, and a door at the opposite side of the room evidently led into the bathroom. She put her luggage down and stood where she was for a moment. She felt like flinging herself down on one of those beds and passing out. She badly needed something to eat or to help her over her nausea. The air-conditioner hummed softly, and a discreet little notice attached to the side of the small refrigerator advised guests to keep doors and windows closed to exclude heat and insects.

Farrell wondered if she should make herself some coffee. But more than coffee, she needed a little brandy to settle her queasy stomach.

She wondered afterwards how she had made such a mistake, but instead of going to the cocktail bar, she took the wrong turning, and walked from another shaded verandah into the saloon bar.

It was crowded with men. There was not a single woman to be seen except for the girl behind the bar. Feeling stunned, Farrell started to cross the floor. Her progress was accompanied by a series of whistles, loud remarks, and invitations. 'What're you doing tonight, love?'—'Hey, honey, what's your name?'—'Come 'n give us a kiss, sweetheart.' Her head spun, someone caught at her arm and she pulled herself free. She was beginning to feel frightened, and she didn't know whether to go on or try to get back out of the room. After hesitating a moment she pushed her way on, keeping her eyes on the blonde barmaid. She reached the bar at last, but before she could even ask for a brandy, there were at least half a dozen men pressing around her offering to buy her a drink. It was like a nightmare and she wished she could wake from it. Somehow a fight broke out, and, badly frightened now, she tried to push her way through the crowd of jostling males and get to the door. She thought she was going to faint, and she almost screamed when hard fingers gripped her arm.

Then a voice she knew said firmly, 'Come on, I've got you, Farrell. Keep moving.'

It was Larry Sandfort.

CHAPTER FOUR

THE next few minutes were hazy, and then she was leaning back on the lounge in a spacious room—one of the suites kept for VIPs from the mining company, she discovered later, in this case, Larry Sandfort.

He held a glass to her lips and she sipped not brandy, but whisky.

'What the hell were you doing along in the saloon bar?' he grated.

Farrell raised her eyes and looked at him. She had met him only once, yet his broad shoulders, that lock of brown hair over his forehead, the softening cleft in his chin—they looked so familiar and so reassuring and they made her feel so safe. The only unrecognisable thing was the expression in his eyes. They were harder than she remembered, more enigmatic, and even more searching.

'I—I needed a brandy,' she said weakly. 'I wasn't feeling well.'

'So? Couldn't someone else have fetched you a brandy? Don't you know it's asking for trouble for a pretty girl—in fact, for practically any woman even remotely personable—to saunter into a roomful of men in a mining town like Ansell?'

'I made a mistake. I—I meant to go to the cocktail bar.' Farrell handed him back the glass and he looked at her narrowly.

'I'd have thought your boy-friend could have got you a brandy, or at least come with you.'

She stared at him, colour rushing to her face. He couldn't possibly have seen her arrive with that truck driver and thought it was her boy-friend—and neither could he possibly know anything about Mark. She said confusedly, 'I'm here on my own. I'm——'

'*Are* you? I'm surprised to find you here at all. According to your father, you're in Port Hedland looking for work.'

Her lashes flicked down. 'Oh. Were you—up there today?'

'That's right. I flew over to the coast early this morning with the specific purpose of doing what I'd told you I was going to do, only to be told you'd gone to Port Hedland.'

'Yes. Well, we—I—I couldn't find work, so we—I——'

'Come on now,' he said roughly, seating himself at the other end of the couch, his body turned so he could look straight at her. 'Which is it going to be? We—or I? You told me a minute ago you're on your own.'

'I am,' she assured him, widening her eyes.

'Are you going to tell me you were referring to the girls you told your father you took off with?'

She looked away from that probing glance. Of course, she could have told him that, but it hadn't entered her head, and now she bit her lip and said nothing.

'Why did you leave home in such a hurry when I told you I'd be back for you, Farrell?' he pressed, dropping the subject.

'You know why—I had to get out of my father's—out of Cecile's hair. Things got—worse. I didn't want to make trouble.'

'You could have hung on and waited for me. You knew I meant what I said.'

Her heart was thudding. Crazily Farrell wished for a moment that she had waited, but she told him, her head up, 'I may be young, but I'm not stupid enough to take up *that* kind of an offer.'

'No?' Through her lashes she saw his lips twist. 'It was

seriously intended, Farrell. I'd have discussed it with your father—received his permission. In my opinion, you did something much more stupid.'

'What—what do you mean?' she stammered.

'What do you think I mean?' His voice had hardened. 'Your stepmother told me—in confidence—that she saw your boy-friend pick you up outside Wesfarmers the morning you left.'

Farrell smothered a gasp. 'All right, but it was only—he just gave me a lift to——'

He stopped her with a gesture of his hand. 'Oh, come on, Farrell. Don't prevaricate or you'll fall over the edge into an outright lie. Why not be honest about what you did? You know damned well it wasn't just a matter of getting a lift. Your stepmother recognised the man as someone named Smith you'd brought to the hotel once. For good measure, she also told me she'd seen you on the beach with him several times—lying about in the sandhills was the way she put it, whatever that might mean.'

'It doesn't mean a thing,' said Farrell huskily. Her pulses were racing. Cecile must have seen her the day Mark chased her, but oh, how unbelievably spiteful, how unfair, to have blown the whole thing up and passed it on to someone who was virtually a stranger—just because she resented Larry Sandfort's interest in her stepdaughter. 'I can't help what Cecile told you. She just doesn't understand.'

'No? Then if it was all so innocent, why didn't you tell your father?' he said dismissively. 'You parted company when you reached Port Hedland, did you?'

'No,' she said, colouring.

'But now you're on your own? When did the alliance break up?'

'Last night. At least—you see, neither of us had found work, so we came through to the tableland, and last night he—I——' she floundered and stopped.

'Go on. What happened last night?'

'Nothing,' she said faintly. 'We—we stayed at a road-house and when I woke up this morning he'd—gone.' Her voice almost faded away as she realised too late how that would sound.

'When you woke up?' he repeated, looking at her incredulously. 'You mean you were sharing a room?'

'It was cheaper,' she said swiftly, and turned away from the dark look in his eyes. Crimson colour surged into her face so that she knew she looked even guiltier than she felt. She knew what conclusions he was drawing from it and hated him for it. She knew too that he wouldn't believe her now if she simply said, 'We didn't sleep together.'

She didn't say it.

'And after all that, he left you,' he commented harshly.

Oh no, Farrell thought bitterly. Not *after* 'all that' at all—*that's* why he left me. She clasped her hands together and pressed them against her knees.

'I hope to heaven you won't discover you're pregnant,' he said after a second.

Farrell nearly died of shame. '*No*,' she said huskily. 'You see, I——'

'Spare me the details. I'll accept you know how to look after yourself—it appears to be something that's taught in primary school these days.' His eyes roamed over her speculatively and she shielded her eyes with her lashes. 'You know, I had the mistaken idea you were a girl with high ideals ... I'm damned sure your father would be shocked if he knew what you've been up to. I'll give you the benefit of the doubt and presume it's your first adventure of this kind. You should be grateful to your stepmother for keeping her information to herself, by the way.'

'Should I?' Her face had paled. 'I rather thought she'd passed it on to you.'

'To me, yes, but not to your father ... Well, I don't like

to be fooled by a girl of nineteen or so, so I appreciate having been put in the picture. I looked for you in Port Hedland, you know—but I begin to wonder if I should have looked for Mr and Mrs Smith in the hotel registers ... Where's he gone? Back to Port Hedland?'

Farrell shrugged as if she didn't know. She felt utterly deflated.

'And what are *your* plans?'

'I—I thought I might get work here.'

'What? After being nearly torn apart in the bar? Have some sense, Farrell!'

'I could do office work,' she said with an attempt at dignity. 'I thought perhaps you could use your influence,' she added, though she was not at all hopeful about that now. 'People must take some notice of what you say——'

'You're the one who'd better take some notice of what I say, Farrell,' he said after a moment. 'I've met your father, I like and respect him, and for that reason alone I wouldn't offer you work in Ansell. You may be tougher than I thought, but you're not *that* tough. No, you can think again.'

Her forehead creased childishly and she ran her fingers nervously through her short bright curls, unaware of exactly how young and defenceless she looked.

'Well, I can't go back home. Cecile and I just don't seem to get along.'

His cynical smile suggested he now had some sympathy with Cecile in that direction. 'Perhaps you're ready after your adventures to take up your university course again. You'll have a few experiences to write about in your spare time.'

Farrell didn't answer. Her adventures had been very different from what he imagined—she appeared to be the sort of girl who screamed at the very thought of sex. What would he make of that? she wondered?

'You're looking green,' he commented. 'Are you feeling ill?'

'I'm—hungry,' she managed with a pale smile.

'Then you'd better tidy yourself up and come and eat with me in the dining room. I'll see if I can muster a few ideas relevant to your future.'

Such as what? she wondered some minutes later as, back in room twenty-four, she rummaged through her luggage in search of something to wear. It was—funny to think back now to that other idea he'd had about her future. She had been in a predicament then and she was in one now, but the whole scene had shifted. He wasn't going to say, 'Marry me' tonight, that was for sure. Of course, she'd have said no, yet perversely she was upset about it. Her—her *amour-propre* was hurt.

As she pulled on a silky high-necked skivvy over a pair of pale oatmeal cotton pants, she felt positive that the only suggestion he would make over dinner was that she should take the plane back to Perth. But she would make up her own mind about that. She was certainly not going to allow him to think he could run her life . . .

The subject of her future wasn't immediately breached at dinner that night, and for that she was thankful. Hunger and weariness made her disinclined to wrestle with the subject, and she was satisfied to sit at the small table with Larry Sandfort eating food that was beautifully cooked and attractively presented, discussing only such matters as what she would have to eat and what wine she would like.

'The food is very good,' she remarked as she finished her flounder.

'Oh yes—everything's the best in Ansell. Compensation for isolation and being deprived of the diversions offered by city life.'

Farrell glanced about her. 'Do all these people work here?'

'The majority of them. Some are tourists, here for a night or two. They'll go out to the gorges or up to the mine and then move on. There's nothing much for them here otherwise.'

Farrell observed that many of the tables were occupied solely by men, most of them wearing good-looking clothes of a casual type, and she was aware that she was the object of interested looks from several quarters. If she had come in alone, without doubt she'd soon have had someone asking to share her table. Well, why not? Her glance lingered on a tanned young man with shining dark hair who was staring at her openly. He looked nice. It could be pleasant to dine and talk with him—maybe to dance later on the tiny circle of parquet flooring that was for that purpose.

As if he had read her thoughts, Larry Sandfort leaned towards her to say sardonically, 'He wouldn't be satisfied merely to eat or to dance with you, Farrell. He'd ask you back to the single men's quarters afterwards. There you'd be flattered, given a few drinks—there's a very well stocked bottle shop in Ansell—and then he'd expect you to go to bed with him.'

And did Larry think she would? She tilted her chin and told him with heightened colour, 'You're a cynic. He—he's probably just a nice ordinary guy.'

'Of course he is. But he's not living in a nice ordinary town. He's lonely, he's badly in need of female company. All the women here are other men's wives.' He reached for his wine glass. 'Well, what's in your mind? Are you going back to Perth?'

She shook her head. 'I want to stay in the North-West. I like it here—it's where I was born. It was just—circumstances beyond my control that took me to the city. Now I'm old enough to decide for myself.'

'I'd question that.' His eyes explored hers. 'Any bright ideas you have you'd better submit to me before you attempt to rush ahead with them. I don't get the impression you're all that inclined towards good sense.'

'I'm not all that inclined towards rashness either,' she retorted swiftly. 'Like agreeing to marry someone I've only just met.'

His nostrils whitened. 'I didn't ask you to do that by any means. However, it's a subject no longer under discussion. We're now concerned with what you're going to do having left university, left your father's home, run away with a man and apparently been deserted by him.'

Farrell recoiled slightly. That was an uncompromising summary of her situation! She said coolly, '*I'll* work it out, Mr Sandfort. I'm grateful to you for coming to my rescue this afternoon, but it doesn't mean I need your help in working out my future.' She finished her coffee—they had both declined dessert—and got up from the table. 'Please excuse me now. Goodnight.'

He got up and walked with her to the exit. She turned her head and gave him a swift look. 'I'm tired. I'm going to bed.'

'I'll see you safely to your door,' he said firmly.

Neither of them spoke again. They went through the door and crossed the garden around the swimming pool. Palm trees cast black shadows on the grass, and above, the stars were sharply silver. No one was sitting at the outdoor tables, the whole courtyard was deserted. They reached Farrell's door and she turned the key, then reached inside for the light switch.

'I'm safe now, Mr Sandfort.'

'My name is still Larry,' he said coolly, and she saw him smile equally coolly. 'Goodnight, Farrell. See you stay safe. Give some thought to your future tonight. I shall.'

'You needn't bother,' she retorted. 'The only way you could help is to recommend me for office work here. And you won't do that.'

'No, I shan't,' he agreed. 'So get it right out of your head.'

She stepped inside and closed the door with a sharp finality, and stood alone in her room.

What *was* she going to do?

'I just don't know,' she said to the impersonal, immaculate, whitewashed walls.

She felt dead tired, but when she looked in the mirror there was a spark of colour in her cheeks.

She rose late in the morning and went to the dining room half expecting to find Larry waiting for her there. Breakfast was almost over. A few people who looked like tourists lingered at a long table talking together. Farrell glanced around cautiously, but the handsome boy who had stared at her so openly last night was not there. A waitress came to take her order, and she asked for toast and marmalade. There were cereals, bowls of canned fruits and jugs of fruit juice at a side table, as well as a coffee urn, hot water, and tea bags.

She helped herself to grapefruit juice, poured a cup of coffee, and went back to the table she had shared last night with Larry. The waitress was a tall young woman of about thirty with a curtain of synthetic blonde hair and a wedding ring on her finger.

'Does your husband work in Ansell?' Farrell asked her with a smile.

'Yes, up at the mine. We've been here nearly two years. We're saving to buy a home down south.'

'I expect the money's good.'

'It would want to be! There's nothing much to do unless you play sports, and I don't. But you get used to it. It either gets you in or you hate it. Are you leaving today?'

'Probably,' said Farrell. She hadn't actually thought it out, she'd fallen asleep too quickly last night to do the thinking Larry Sandfort had urged. But now, somehow—

since he wasn't here—she felt an urge to get out.

'You must be going on the plane,' said the waitress, beginning to clear the next table. 'You aren't with the tourists who came on the coach, are you? Didn't you dine with Larry Sandfort last night?'

'Yes.' Farrell coloured slightly. 'He's a friend of my father's,' she said rather pointlessly. 'Do you know if he's breakfasted yet?'

'Sure—some time ago. He's gone down to the conference room at the offices. There's discussions about building self-contained quarters for the single men—some of them don't like the communal dining room and they come here. The VIPs are divided. They'll be sorting it out all day, more than likely.'

Farrell smiled, then asked as the girl began to move away with a loaded tray, 'By the way, what time does the plane go?'

'To Port Hedland, you mean? There's no plane for Perth today. So it would be around eleven-thirty.'

Farrell thanked her for the information. Well, she might as well go to Port Hedland, she thought wearily. It would be a start, and it looked as if she'd have to get out of here anyhow.

In her room some minutes later she used the telephone to get through to Ansell Air Services.

'Yes, that'll be okay,' said the pleasant male voice. 'What's the name?'

'Fitzgerald—Miss Fitzgerald.'

'Oh—hang on.' There was a brief silence, then, 'Hello? Look here, Miss Fitzgerald, I'm afraid it's not possible to let you have a seat after all.'

'But—but you just said it would be all right,' she exclaimed incredulously.

'I'm sorry, I made a mistake. The plane's booked out.'

'Then tomorrow,' she insisted, after a second's thought.

'I'm sorry, nothing doing tomorrow.'

'But that's ridiculous! The Perth plane, then——'

'Afraid not. Your best bet would be to see—er—one of the VIPs.'

'Such as Mr Sandfort,' snapped Farrell, and slammed the receiver down furiously. It was perfectly plain that Larry Sandfort had given orders she was not to leave on the plane—she was to submit her plans to him before she rushed into anything! She felt helplessly angry. In this company-owned town, it seemed there was no limit to the power of the directors. But not over *her*. She would tell Larry Sandfort the minute she saw him that she was not going to submit to this interference. He had no right to make her even a temporary prisoner in this town. It wasn't even as if he wanted to marry her—oh, heavens, no! He had completely changed his mind about that! 'That's a subject no longer under discussion,' he had said ...

She discovered she was sitting in the chair staring at the wall behind the telephone, and that her thoughts had brought a dew of perspiration to her top lip despite the air-conditioning. Yet she most certainly didn't want to discuss that subject!

A little later, she put on sunglasses and went for a stroll around the town, marvelling again at the greenery and lushness of gardens and parks that had been established less than eight years. The town lay in a saucer, ringed about with red ironstone hills, but there was no sign of the mine.

In the modern shopping complex, she bought herself a sandwich and a carton of fresh orange juice and went to sit in the park, and later spent an hour or so in the cool of the library she found tucked away behind the poinciana trees. Around three o'clock she emerged to find the sun burningly hot and as she walked back to the hotel the glare was almost intolerable despite her sunglasses. The surrounding hills threw back the heat from their ironstone caps and crows flew overhead uttering their harsh and gruesome cries. Suddenly this green, man-made oasis in the middle of the semi-desert seemed a hostile place, close to hell.

'I should never get used to it,' Farrell thought, and she felt furious that Larry Sandfort had blocked her from leaving even while he wouldn't let her work there. If he thought he was entitled to keep her prisoner while he decided what was to be done about her future, he was greatly mistaken. She quickened her step.

She was swimming up and down the hotel pool when she discovered he had returned. Actually, she was afraid to get out of the water because that handsome boy of last night had come with a group of others to sit drinking at one of the tables, and not one of them had taken their eyes off her. Consequently, it was a tremendous relief to see Larry. He came to stand at the edge of the pool, and she swam over to him.

'How many laps does that make, Farrell?' he asked, raising one eyebrow. 'What are you trying to do? Get into the Guinness Book of Records? Come on, you've had enough exercise. Where's your towel?'

'It's over there,' she said, her teeth chattering through nervousness. 'There' was by that group of men, and Larry gave her a narrow-eyed look before he strode across the lawn, gathered up her towel and returned to where she was scrambling out of the water. Nobody else had been swimming, and she felt conspicuous and self-conscious in her black bikini.

He wrapped the towel around her, his warm fingers touching her bare flesh, and she drew away quickly.

'Go and get dressed,' he told her. 'I'll be in the cocktail lounge.'

She took her time, washing her hair under the shower and drying it thoroughly before she got into a long cotton dress sprigged with tiny flowers and pinched in at the waist with a wide elastic belt. She used moisturising cream and a touch of lipstick and decided she didn't need eye-shadow—there were dark smudges under her eyes as it was. She'd been having a gruesome time lately, what with one thing and another.

'Well, how did you put in the day?' he asked when she joined him. He had already ordered a gin squash for her and she slid on to the stool beside him at the bar and reached for it thirstily. Her eyes flashed green as she told him accusingly, 'Trying to get out of your town, Mr Sand-fort.'

He smiled slightly. 'I thought you might do that. And it didn't strike me as being a good idea.'

'You had no right to stop me,' she retorted. 'I—I hate this town. It's like a furnace. It's full of crows, and I get a creepy-crawly feeling they're waiting to pick my bones if I stay here.'

He actually laughed. 'So you've changed your mind about the North-West, have you?'

'About this part of it,' she agreed. '*Your* part. I've been thanking my lucky stars all day I didn't fall for that line you gave me—I'd never forgive myself if I'd landed *here* to do a crash course with you.'

'Is that so?' His eyes had hardened. 'And have you managed to forgive yourself for what you *did* do?'

Her cheeks went scarlet. 'You don't know a thing about that. It's not—not under discussion.'

His eyebrows rose, but he made no comment on that. 'However, I didn't ask you to come *here*, Farrell, I said I'd take you to Quindalup, which is a very different proposition.'

'Is it? Well, I couldn't really care less.'

He changed the subject entirely. 'Do you need another drink, or are you ready for dinner?'

'I'm ready for dinner. But—but I don't want to have it with you.'

'I think you'd better,' he said. 'However, if it will make you feel happier, the charge can be added to your account.'

Farrell bit her lip. Her money was fast disappearing and she would have to ask her father to send her a cheque soon or she would be in trouble. She declined another drink, slid down from the stool and went in to dinner with him.

'Tomorrow, I'll take you up to have a look at Mount Ansell,' he said as they were eating.

'I might not want to go,' she said unco-operatively.

'Now don't tell me that, Farrell. It's all grist for a writer's mill.'

She looked at him through her lashes uncertain how to take it. She didn't say so, but she knew she would give in and go with him. What else was there to do when he wouldn't let her take the plane and disappear from Ansell? She didn't like him, she decided, yet—oh, she didn't know *what* she felt . . .

Deliberately, the following morning, she didn't breakfast with him, but later she presented herself at the hour he had nominated. She half expected him to praise her for being sensible, but he did no such thing and took her presence for granted. He saw her into the front seat of a dusty-looking four-wheel-drive vehicle, then took the driver's seat and drove out of the town. As they passed a flourishing park, she wondered how all this plant life was supported. Travelling with Mark, and later wth George, she had crossed many rivers, and every one of them had been dry—sandy beds with trees growing there. Where did the water come from to make all those gardens grow in Ansell—to keep all those houses supplied?

She asked Larry.

'It's piped from bores sunk in the bed of the Fortescue

River,' he told her. 'Don't you know that the water of most of our rivers is under the ground? Haven't you been to Carnavon where the banana plantations are watered from dry river beds?'

'I haven't been anywhere much,' she admitted. 'Perth and up on the coast——'

'And currently you've been walkabout in the Pilbara,' he said coolly. 'But you don't like my part of the world.'

She moved uncomfortably. Actually, she found the Pilbara fascinating. It had been the glare—those crows—the feeling of being trapped that had shaken her. Now it gave her a tremendous thrill to be driving into ranges that looked older than time, to see them floating ahead mauve and pink and unreal, with heavenly blue shadows deepening to indigo in their clefts, but she didn't feel like enthusing to Larry and merely said reservedly, 'I wouldn't say that, exactly. But—but don't most people find it hard to live here? Even in Ansell, where there's—everything—people don't stay long, do they? George told me the labour turnover's terribly high.'

'George?' She saw his face darken. 'Who's that? Your boy-friend?'

'No. Just a—a man who gave me a lift,' she said nervously.

'Good God!' He muttered something else under his breath, then told her grimly, 'You'll write to your father tonight. You'll tell him that you've left Port Hedland and are now in my care.'

Farrell sent him a wry look, but he didn't see it. She couldn't really believe that her father would be reassured by that kind of news, and heaven knew what Cecile would think!

'Well?' he said sharply.

'Well what?'

'Do you agree to write?'

'No, of course I don't.'

'Then I shall have to make you write. There's nothing admirable about young runaways who worry their parents sick by failing to keep reasonably in touch. Doesn't it bother you that your father may be concerned about your safety and wellbeing?'

'I've already written to my father,' she said curtly.

'And what did you tell him?'

'There was nothing to tell—just that I hadn't found work——'

'Well, you'll write another letter tonight. In fact, I'll dictate it to you and you'll write what I say.'

'Dictating's one of your strong points, isn't it? Like dictating to me that I'm not to be allowed to fly out of Ansell. Well, I don't like being dictated to—I'm just glad I didn't wait about at my father's for you to come back. I just might have been carried off to Quindalup whether I wanted it or not.'

'That's something that could still happen,' he said sardonically, and Farrell glared at his profile as the four-wheel-drive hurtled along the gravel road.

'I hardly think so. You've made it plain that's all off.'

'I've made it plain you've shattered the opinion I formed of you when we met initially.'

Her colour flared. 'Then isn't it all quite simple? Let me go and forget about me.'

'I wish he could,' he said after a moment. 'Unfortunately, I have a conscience—a sense of responsibility. The way I see it, you've taken a reckless step in the dark and you've fallen over the edge of a precipice. I prefer to help you back from the very narrow ledge you're resting on rather than see you slip further down. Do you get my point?'

'I'm not going to—slip further down,' Farrell said tightly. 'In fact, Mr Sandfort, though it may surprise you, I—I haven't fallen over the edge at all. You just don't understand——'

'I understand all right, Farrell,' he said grimly. 'Perhaps

we see things differently. But I do know it's never so hard to take the second false step as it is to take the first, and if you've found the first step easy—well——' He shrugged, and the discussion, if it could be called that, ended there, for they had reached the security gates of Ansell-Sandfort Mining.

Once inside, they were both required to conform with regulations and were provided with yellow helmets and big sunglasses to protect their eyes. Soon, Larry was driving the dusty four-wheel-drive up a wide graded road into the mountain, and Farrell was glad to forget personalities and allow her natural interest to take over.

She had expected dust in these bare red mountains that were being mined for their rich iron ore, but water trucks rumbled up and down the road constantly, spraying the surface to keep the dust to a minimum, and despite the heat it was not unpleasant.

'As you see, we use the conventional open-pit mining methods on Mount Ansell,' Larry told her as they drove towards the pit observation point. 'Roughly speaking, the ore is blasted out of the ground, scooped up and loaded into trucks, then carried to the crushers you probably noticed down below. There it's screened and stockpiled, and finally taken by company rail to the port.'

Farrell nodded, listening absorbedly. At the observation point, high on the rocky mountainside that reflected back the glare of the sun, she climbed out at Larry's invitation to see what was going on. Some distance down, huge diesel-electric shovels were loading ore into dump-trucks. From this height they looked tiny, men were no more than ants, yet Larry said the shovels collected fifteen tonnes of ore at a single bite, and that the trucks carting the ore carried a hundred tonnes in a load. Everything was red, except for the yellow of the machinery and the men's helmets, and far below the tiny brilliant splash of a grassy park. This had been planted for psychological reasons, and as well to relieve the men's eyes.

Farrell understood now why so many of the men she had seen in town looked as if the red of the iron was ground into their tanned skins. It actually was. She could understand too why they didn't stay too long working at Mount Ansell.

She glanced at the man standing by her side, staring out over the great project that had started as a dream in one man's mind before it had ever become a reality. He was almost totally unrecognisable in his yellow helmet, the big glasses covering the upper part of his face and giving him the air of a man from outer space. She suppressed a smile at the thought that she must look pretty weird too, as he turned towards her to ask, 'Are you interested? Or is it too masculine a world for you?'

'It is masculine—fearsomely so,' she admitted. 'But it's fascinating—exciting,' she added, half beneath her breath.

'I almost expected to hear you let out a little female wail of pity because we're pulling a mighty mountain to bits.'

Farrell looked out thoughtfully over the immensity of ancient spinifex-dotted ranges that rippled and snaked, empty and desolate, away to the horizon and beyond. In that eternal landscape, the mining operations on Mount Ansell looked utterly insignificant.

'It's really a very *small* mountain, isn't it?' she commented. 'It's funny—it's a huge project to us, yet it's making no more than a tiny scar. We're like ants with our earthworks.'

He smiled a little. 'Then you're not unduly depressed by this desecration of the earth.'

She shook her head. 'I guess man has to use the minerals he finds. Our civilisation's founded on what we got out of the ground.'

Larry reached out and rested a hand casually on her

shoulder. 'You'll be reaching for your notebook in a moment, Farrell.'

'My—notebook?' she repeated.

'Surely every would-be writer has a notebook! That was one reason why I brought you here—to add a different type of experience, of earthiness, to the kind you've been investigating for yourself.'

Farrell didn't have to work out what that was supposed to mean, but she wondered what he would think if he knew how she had reacted to that other kind of earthy experience.

She turned away, the moment spoiled by this intrusion of the personal, and made her way back to the Landrover.

He followed her, and asked casually as he got into the driver's seat, 'Were you in love with the man you went away with? Or was it all in the nature of an adventure?'

He looked at her as he spoke, and she looked back at him, but it was like looking at a mask. She couldn't discover his eyes behind the lashes, and the expression on his mouth was cynical. She said wearily, 'It wasn't an adventure. I was looking for work.'

'And my other question,' he said after a moment. 'Were you in love with him?'

Farrell hesitated. She had liked Mark at first. Now she didn't know what she felt about him. Perhaps it would sound better if she said yes, but it would not be true. She sighed. 'Does it matter? I don't really have to answer your questions. It's not as if——'

'Not as if we were back to square one? No, things have changed somewhat, haven't they?'

She bent her head. 'You should have let me go yesterday.'

'Perhaps I should.' Larry started up the motor and they began to descend the mountain.

CHAPTER FIVE

FARRELL was thankful when Larry told her later that he was going out to dinner that night, but she was chagrined when she went to the dining room to discover he had arranged for her to sit at a table occupied by two middle-aged couples doing a tour of the North-West.

Dinner over, she went straight to her room. He had said she was to write to her father, and she had no doubt he would pounce on her and check up in the morning. Well, she would have a letter written, signed, and sealed, and what was in it was no concern of his. She wasn't like Mark—she didn't want to worry her father.

She found it difficult to compose a letter because of all the tricky points involved—how she happened to be in Ansell, what she was now doing there, what her future plans were—— She simply didn't dare mention Larry Sandfort, she could imagine what Cecile would make of *that*, if she found it so easy to make something suggestive of the harmless relationship that had existed between Farrell and Mark.

After some thought, she wrote, 'Dear Daddy, I thought I had better let you know where I am. I got tired of trying to find work in Port Hedland and now I'm in Ansell, and haven't quite made up my mind what to do next.' That written, she sat staring at the wall and wondering futilely about what else she could say. From there, her thoughts strayed to Mark, who didn't write home, and she wondered where he was now and what he was doing, and what he thought about the girl who had led him on and then reneged. Oh yes, Farrell had to admit she had given him the wrong impression when she had asked if she could come with him. He had probably wiped her from his mind now—he'd never pretended to be madly in love with her, or anything like that. In fact, she didn't think Mark would classify as being a passionate sort of person. Not like Larry Sandfort. All the same, it didn't look as if Farrell Fitzgerald needed to run to protect herself from Larry these days!

The telephone rang and she jumped about a foot.

'Farrell? This is Larry. Come over to the TV room, will you, and we'll discuss that letter you're going to write.'

'I don't need to discuss it with you,' Farrell said promptly, and with a little feeling of triumph. 'I've written it already,' she added, stretching the truth slightly.

'Have you? Well, I'd like to see it.' He paused and Farrell said nothing. She merely seethed with resentment. Wasn't this an—an invasion of privacy? 'Either you bring it along or I come to your room,' he said when she didn't answer. 'I'll give you five minutes.'

He rang off and Farrell hung up. She looked at her letter and grimaced. It wasn't worth showing to anybody. She tore it slowly to shreds. She would have to go to the TV room, she supposed—she certainly didn't want him coming here. She would see what suggestions he had to make, but quite definitely she wasn't going to sit down and meekly write what he dictated. She combed out her curls and looked at herself critically in the mirror. She was wearing a long cotton dress, and she looked terribly young and more than a little lost, and that was exactly how she felt.

When she reached the TV room it was crowded with viewers, all of them laughing their heads off over the Garry MacDonald show, and Larry Sandfort was waiting by the door.

'I'm sorry about this, Farrell. This show's just started—I looked in here before I phoned you and there wasn't a soul in sight.' He took her arm. 'We'll have to go to my suite.

It's too noisy in the bar, and it's too cool outside. You'd catch a chill in that thin dress.'

Farrell held back. 'I don't want to go to your suite. If you just tell me what you want me to say, I'll manage without bothering you—though I'm not saying I'll write it.'

He raised his eyebrows. 'I don't particularly want you to come to my suite either, if that's what's bothering you. Could be that what you've already written will pass. Have you got your letter there? Let me take a look——'

She coloured. 'I—I tore it up. I wasn't satisfied.'

'Obviously you need a little help.' His blue eyes flicked over her face and lingered on her mouth, then abruptly he turned away. 'Come along.' He didn't take her arm again, and they walked without touching each other through the courtyard past the swimming pool. He ushered her politely into his suite, and she took the chair he indicated. There was a lamp on a low table and another on the cocktail cabinet, and Larry reached for cigarettes and offered one to Farrell before he sat down. She shook her head, and remarked as he lit up, 'I didn't know you smoked.'

'I don't as a rule. Only under stress.' He smiled briefly, his teeth white against the tan of his face.

Under stress! Farrell would have thought *she* was the one under stress!

'Why are you under stress?' she wanted to know.

'I'm carrying it over from the business dinner I attended,' he said lightly, and Farrell looked at him through her lashes as he sat down facing her. Was that true? She was not too sure.

'Don't look at me like that,' he said sharply.

'Like—like what?'

'Like a woman summing a man up,' he said tersely.

She opened her eyes wide and smiled ingenuously. 'I *was* summing you up.'

Their eyes met and now in Larry's there was exactly the

expression Farrell had seen in them when she had first met him—that expression that had so fascinated and intrigued her. She found it difficult, in fact almost impossible, to look away from him. Finally he was the one to break the spell, moving impatiently to reach for an ashtray, and ashing his cigarette with unnecessary deliberation.

'Have you a pen?' he asked. 'A writing pad?'

She had neither, and he got up and found both for her.

'Now let's see—what do you call your father?'

She didn't answer, but she wrote, 'Dear Daddy,' noting uneasily that her writing was uneven. She glanced up expectantly, and found him looking at her searchingly, and she nervously took a handful of her fair hair and dragged at it.

Larry asked unexpectedly, 'Are those curls natural?'

'Yes—they're an awful nuisance sometimes. I have to wear my hair cut short or it's impossible. I can't even think of following hair fashions.'

'Why should you want to when you can look like that?'

'Like—like what?' she stammered.

Instead of answering he got to his feet and paced across the room. 'Good God, Farrell,' he said, his back to her, 'you surely must be aware how attractive you are. You *look* naïve—but you're obviously not. Didn't the man you ran away with pay you compliments?' He swung round and came to take her chin roughly and tilt her face up to his. 'Didn't he tell you your eyes are like—dreaming waters where ferns grow—that you have the lips and the bosom of a houri? Didn't he want to kiss your lovely hair, to——' He stopped abruptly, releasing her, his eyes lingering on her breast which by now was rising and falling quickly with her quickened breathing. What was this a prelude to?

She heard herself breathe out, 'Leave me alone! I wish you'd—I wish you'd just let me go my own way——'

'Your own way? What is your own way?' he asked sav-

agely. He flung himself into a chair and his eyes smould-
ered at her. 'I'm going to see that you count to more than
ten before you set out on another journey, Farrell ... Come
on now, let's get this letter written. Tell your father this—
that Larry Sandfort's offered you sanctuary at Quindalup,
his hideout in the gorges, while you make up your mind
whether you want to go back to university or become a
writer or a secretary or whatever. Tell him that I'm going
to keep an eye on you.'

They stared at each other, Farrell motionless though her
heart was thudding, the man grim-lipped, his eyes dark,
thought some fire burned in their depths. The thought of
going to Quindalup—or anywhere at all—with him terrified
her, though she was not sure why. The thing was—how did
you know what to expect of a man? She had thought herself
so safe with Mark——

'I—don't want to go to Quindalup,' she said huskily.
'You talk as if I have to do what you say—as if I have no
choice——'

He crushed out his forgotten cigarette. 'You don't have a
choice. I promise you, you can't get out of this town unless
you walk—and you know damned well you'd have to be out
of your senses to do that.'

Farrell's cheeks felt pinched, and she knew they were
white. 'You're made of iron like your mountains, aren't
you?'

'Do you think so? ... Now write your letter, Miss Fitzgerald, and when it's done, I'll check it—and I'll post it.'

'All right.' Farrell rose and crossed to the desk and took
the chair there. There was a wall mirror in front of her and
she could see him in it—lighting another cigarette, his head
lowered, the light flaring warmly on the strong planes of his
face. She began to write quickly, intent of getting it over,
'Dear Daddy, I thought I'd better let you know I'm in
Ansell. I couldn't find anything to do in Port Hedland so

decided to take a look at the mountains. The money has been holding out and I hate to ask you for more, but I'd appreciate it if you could let me have a cheque, just as a standby. Do you remember Mr Sandfort who was staying at the hotel a while ago? I've run into him. It appears he practically owns Ansell, and he's kindly said I could——'

She stopped writing and raised her eyes to the mirror to meet Larry's blue gaze. 'What did you say I was to tell my father about Quindalup?'

'What have you written so far?'

Without asking her permission he moved forward and took up the page she had been writing on. When he had read it he looked at her quizzically.

'That's very convincing—all milk and water. Your step-mother may find it amusing, but for her own sake I don't think she'll communicate her amusement to your father.'

'She just might,' Farrell retorted. She already knew Cecile's opinion of Larry, and didn't imagine she would consider Farrell in safe hands. 'Anyhow, my father will be furious if he finds out you've as good as kidnapped me.'

'He might be even angrier if he knows what else you've been up to.' He tossed the sheet of paper down. 'Carry on. Mr Sandfort *kindly* said you could have the use of his— let's see, holiday home might sound better than hideout. Have you got that?' He looked over her shoulder. 'Then you'd better indicate that you mean to take the opportunity to think seriously about your future plans.'

'I've come to a sort of standstill,' Farrell wrote after a little thought, 'and I need a few days to think about my next move. Don't worry about me, Daddy. I'll keep in touch and I shan't do anything silly. Goodbye for now, lots of love from Farrell.'

Larry read that through too, as she had known he would, and she saw his lips twist in a slight smile.

'That's a lie I've told on your account, Mr Sandfort,' she

told him. 'I know I'm doing a very silly thing in letting you push me around, but I don't seem to have a great deal of choice at the moment. I don't know what my father will think.'

'You'd better add a postscript,' he said dryly. 'Mr Sandfort is going to keep an eye on you—a strict eye,' he amended.

Farrell dispensed with the 'strict', then sealed and addressed the envelope and handed it over with a grimace.

'You don't trust me, do you? Yet you expect me to trust you.'

'I haven't given you any reason not to, have I?'

'Not yet,' she said, and added emphatically, 'But I don't want to go to Quindalup. Why should I?—particularly as I don't know a thing about it.'

'You'll have plenty of time to find out all you want—starting from tomorrow.' He narrowed his eyes and moved towards the cocktail cabinet. 'You look like you could do with a drink. Will gin and tonic do?'

Farrell stood up nervously. 'I don't want a drink, thank you.'

His eyes were mocking. 'I don't mean to get you senseless and seduce you. You're perfectly safe, Farrell, so sit down and stop acting like a frightened virgin.'

She coloured furiously and perched on the edge of an armchair. It appeared that when Larry insisted on something, there was no escape. He was certainly accustomed to having his orders obeyed. She watched him nervily as he poured her drink, and a whisky for himself.

'Cheers,' he said when he had passed her glass across. 'We'll leave tomorrow afternoon, by the way, so see you're packed up.'

Farrell chewed her lower lip. So he was coming too. The fact didn't reassure her.

'Is there—is there anyone else at Quindalup?'

'Don't worry. My housekeeper's there, and she's a very efficient woman.'

Farrell swallowed down half her drink. 'I'd much rather leave on the plane tomorrow.'

'And shoot another arrow into the air? No, don't argue, you'll do as I say.'

Her hand was shaking, and it was as much from anger as from anything else. 'Why can't you just let me go?'

'Oh, quit acting like a butterfly that's being threatened with a pin! I've told you why. I don't want to see you ruin your life.'

'I imagined you thought I'd done that already,' she retorted swiftly.

Larry smiled crookedly. 'Not altogether. It's just that I'm a little old-fashioned.'

'I don't need your patronage anyhow!'

'Nevertheless you've got it—if you choose to call it patronage.'

'Oh!' she exclaimed in sudden frustration. She jumped up and banged down the glass on the cabinet top so forcefully that it shattered. She drew her hand up quickly, aware that she had cut her finger, and stared at the drops of blood beginning to form, then at the fragments of glass on the shining cabinet top. 'I'm sorry—I didn't mean to do that.'

Larry moved as she spoke, and before she was aware of it he had taken hold of her hand and carried it to his mouth. She felt the warmth of his tongue as he sucked the blood from her finger. Somehow shocked, she pulled her hand away as if he had done something unforgivable, only to have her wrist captured and to find herself jerked almost off balance as he drew her against him.

She raised her head and stared straight into the blue of his eyes, then his gaze moved slowly to her mouth and her senses spun. The next moment, without being aware of what she was doing, she was fighting him like a wild creature.

He uttered an exclamation and released her so suddenly and so completely that she fell into the chair behind her. While she sat there trying to control her breathing, he turned away and, somehow infuriatingly, poured himself another drink and tossed it down his throat. Farrell, her breast rising and falling, was asking herself wretchedly, 'Why on earth did I do that?' She had no real idea except that she was frightened at the thought of having him kiss her.

He turned to her and asked abruptly, 'Is that other man still on your mind?'

'Yes,' she breathed out, simply because she didn't know what else to say. She was blinking back tears now, and she refused to look at him. The thought of going to Quindalup with him the next day drove her close to panic. There had to be some way of getting out of it ...

There was no way, of course. Or was it simply a matter of knowing that getting the better of Larry Sandfort was well beyond her capabilities? At all events, they left for Quindalup the following afternoon just as he had ordained, following a narrow gravel road that ran into the ranges and became more and more lonely with every mile. The lower slopes of the ranges were covered with spinifex and the soft mauve of mullamullas, the wildflower that, north of Capricorn, replaced the everlasting daisy of the south.

There was not another vehicle on the road, and the silence and emptiness were intense when finally they reached a sheltered valley into which a narrow gorge opened. Soon, a house came into view, well off the road, its soft colours merging unobtrusively with the surrounding garden and tall eucalypts.

'This is it,' said Larry. 'Quindalup—a happy place, in our language. You'll be able to meditate here.'

'On my sins?' she asked quickly.

'On your future,' he corrected her with a darkly level look.

He pulled up in the shade of some trees some yards from the house, and Farrell looked curiously ahead at the bungalow with its pinkish asbestos roofing and wide verandahs. The garden was crowded with flowering shrubs and native plants, and a well kept lawn swept down to an unexpected stretch of water at the back.

'Don't tell me that's a river!' Farrell exclaimed as she got out of the car and stood staring about her.

'It's not,' said Larry. 'To put it briefly, it's water released from an artesian basin by a fault in the rock formation. You can swim there with perfect safety.' He turned away to get the luggage out of the vehicle, and Farrell saw her two bags appear and nothing else. She felt a small shock of incredulity. Wasn't he staying? She had dreaded the thought of coming here with him, but now—she had a resentful feeling that she was being dumped here—got rid of—left to repent her sins in solitary confinement, while he went back to his life and forgot her.

He motioned to her to go through the garden ahead of him and she hesitated. She felt extraordinarily like throwing a tantrum—a thing she hadn't done since she was a small child. She wanted to stamp her foot and scream and refuse to move—to demand that he take her back to Ansell. She wasn't quite sure why she didn't follow her impulse—whether it was because she knew she'd be ashamed, or for some other reason. At the very back of her mind floated a vague and feathery idea that to reject Quindalup would be to refuse an invitation from fate. Though heaven knew she had no particular reason to trust the invitations fate had been tossing around so open-handedly lately. She'd already landed herself in a whole lot of trouble by taking what had seemed a heaven-sent opportunity to extract herself from her stepmother's life . . .

Meanwhile, she had about-faced and was walking meekly ahead of Larry to the house, and she was aware of a faint sense of enchantment. Beautiful trees cast purple and red shadows on the green of the grass, mullamullas and some of the flowering peas glowed gold and white, pink and mauve and crimson in the bush beyond the paths. Birds called, and against the sky in the background, the red walls of the gorge glowed in the late afternoon sunlight. Quindalup, she thought involuntarily, could be a paradise for—lovers. A romantic and improbable haven, hidden away in a brutal land.

A little shaken by her thoughts, she glanced back over her shoulder and waited for Larry to come abreast of her, reflecting that he looked very much a part of this place—a man completely different from the one in the yellow helmet and concealing glasses, with his healthily tanned skin, his blue eyes, his thick glossy hair.

'Are you—staying?' she heard herself ask, although in her heart she already knew he was not.

Larry gave her a veiled look. 'I'm not in the mood for a holiday.'

'Neither am I,' she retorted, quick colour staining her cheeks.

'Well then, you'll be able to give your whole mind to devising some sensible plans, won't you? You won't be disturbed here.'

'I can see that,' she flashed, and added, with a deliberate rejection of the beauty of Quindalup, 'I'm going to be bored to tears.'

'I hope not,' he said, definitely displeased. 'I'll drive out and see how you're progressing, of course.'

Was she to be grateful for that? Farrell wondered mutinously.

A woman had appeared on the verandah to welcome them. She was fiftyish, tall and thin with a weatherbeaten face and short-cut greying hair, and she was neatly dressed in navy cotton slacks and a matching short-sleeved shirt.

'This is Mrs Adams, my housekeeper,' Larry told Farrell. 'Mrs Adams—Miss Farrell Fitzgerald. I want to leave her in your care for a little while. She's in need of—peace and quiet.'

The two women murmured greetings and Farrell wondered what interpretation Mrs Adams put on what Larry said. He had given the impression that she hadn't been well, or had been in some sort of trouble perhaps, and Farrell hoped she wouldn't be fussed over, but as she discovered she need not have worried about that.

'You won't be staying, Mr Sandfort?' the housekeeper asked, turning to her employer.

'Regrettably, no. I have a dinner appointment in Ansell tonight, and tomorrow Steve Porter has some papers for me to sign. I'll see Miss Fitzgerald settled in and then I must go.'

'You'll have a cup of tea?'

'No, thank you. Make a pot for Miss Fitzgerald by all means, but I shan't wait. Now where would you like this luggage?'

'Oh, I'll see to that, Mr Sandfort. There's a bed ready made up in the second room.' She hastened away with the suitcases and Farrell stood silently feeling like a schoolgirl helpless to resist the plans being made for her.

'Well, Farrell,' said Larry, 'I'm leaving you in good hands, so I'll say goodbye for the time being.'

She sent him a smouldering look. 'I don't want to stay here, you know.'

He raised his eyebrows. 'What's your alternative, then? If you have one, let's hear it. I'm ready to listen.'

'Oh!' she exclaimed, exasperated. 'You have no right to treat me like this. I can—I can do as I please——'

'I've let your father know I'll be responsible for you,' he said imperturbably. 'I'm not leaving you here indefinitely—I shall be back.'

'*When*?' she asked furiously.

'When I've discharged a few of my responsibilities,' he said briefly, and turned away. 'Goodbye, Farrell.'

Farrell had never felt so helpless or so baffled in her life. She watched him turn his car, watched him drive back along the gravel road without so much as a glance in her direction, and then, when the sound of the motor had faded away, the silence came back.

Presently Mrs Adams walked briskly on to the verandah with a tray of tea.

'I've put your things in your bedroom, Miss Fitzgerald— the second door along. You'll find a bathroom across the hallway, and if there's anything at all you want, be sure to tell me. Dinner will be at seven, breakfast at eight-thirty, and lunch at one. Of course if you want to walk up the gorge and take a picnic lunch at any time, you have only to say so and I'll pack a basket for you. You're welcome in the kitchen any time to get yourself a snack or a drink, so don't be shy.'

'Thank you, Mrs Adams,' Farrell said wryly. She was beginning to gain the impression—later proved to be correct—that Larry's housekeeper was highly organised.

Her bedroom, she presently discovered, was spacious and airy, attractively furnished, and equipped, like all the other rooms in the bungalow, with a big ceiling fan, which would be essential once the weather really warmed up. There was ample space for her clothes, and for want of something better to do, she unpacked her suitcases and arranged the things in the drawers and wardrobe, in which, on a pretty padded hanger, hung a silky, very feminine yellow and white striped bathrobe. Who owned that, she wondered, or was it provided for the use of guests? She learned at least part of the answer to her question the following day.

She ate alone that night—in fact she ate all her meals alone, for Mrs Adams didn't mix with guests and kept strictly to her role of housekeeper, and to her own part of the house, which was completely separate. After dinner, Farrell wandered into the big living room in search of some way of entertaining herself, for she didn't intend to spend her time moping or reflecting on her future. There was a radio, and a whole stack of cassette tapes with something to suit every taste. Farrell selected some Chopin waltzes, then wandered over to inspect the row of books on a long shelf that ran half way along one wall. Somewhat to her surprise, among the fiction, history and mineralogy, there were several volumes of poetry—Blake, Hopkins, some Chinese translations, Shakespeare's sonnets. Larry's name was inscribed in all of them, she discovered to her surprise, for she hadn't expected him to be a man who enjoyed verse. At least, she was sure he wouldn't subscribe to Aunt Jean's views, and claim that a Shakespearean sonnet gave him more pleasure than sex!

She shied away from her own thoughts and opened the sonnets and read, 'Shall I compare thee to a summer's day? Thou art more lovely and more temperate——' and into her mind, uncalled for, came something he had said to her recently, remembered now with unexpected vividness. 'Eyes like dreaming waters where ferns grow—the lips and bosom of a houri'... Farrell bit her lip and closed the book and put it back on the shelf. Larry Sandfort was an enigma, and she knew a fleeting and instantly banished regret that she was not staying at Quindalup under different circumstances.

The next morning, some time after breakfast, she decided to take a swim. The sun was hot and the water sparkled invitingly down beyond the trees. Farrell slipped into her bikini, and, on the point of donning her towelling beach coat, reached down instead the silky scrap of robe she had come upon the previous day. It felt cool and caressing against her half-naked body, and she tied the narrow belt, put on her thongs, and headed for the pool.

Beyond the garden as she approached the water, which was overhung by the white branches of snappy gums, she encountered Mrs Adams returning to the house.

'I thought you'd probably take a swim this morning, Miss Fitzgerald. I've put some fresh fruit drink in the little fridge in the sun shelter, and a couple of bottles of soft drink. Help yourself, won't you?'

Farrell thanked her and continued on her way. The sun shelter was a rustic, half open construction, roofed with big sheets of pale papery bark from the cadjeput trees, several of which grew nearby. There were li-los and folding chairs stacked against one of its rough wooden walls, and as well as a small kerosene refrigerator, Farrell noticed a table and a small cabinet of oiled timber. The floor was covered with seagrass matting.

She took one of the li-los outside and set it up close to the water, then absentmindedly thrust her hands into the pockets of her robe. Her right hand encountered something and she drew it out. It was a card—a birthday card—with a design of wildflowers, red and green kangaroo paws, on the front. Inside was a printed greeting under which was scrawled in a strong masculine hand, 'The happiest of birthdays, to my lovely Helen.' It was signed 'Larry'. Farrell felt a curious tingling run along her nerves. 'My lovely Helen'. She looked at the card again, but there was no date, nothing to show when it had been written. Well, what did she care if he had a girl-friend called Helen, who apparently visited Quindalup? She didn't care in the least. She put the card back in her pocket, slipped out of the robe and tossed it down on the li-lo.

No, she didn't care a fig about the girls in Larry Sandfort's life, yet, lazing in the sun-warmed water a few minutes later, she wondered why he hadn't married his lovely Helen. Was she one of the girls he had loved and lost? Had he frightened her off by his bossy ways, his imperiousness? Was it this fault in his make-up that forced him to resort to planned tactics to get himself a wife? No, Farrell didn't manage to convince herself of that. A certain despotism could be an attractive quality in a man, could emphasise his masculinity, and Farrell was well aware that there must have been plenty of girls in his life willing and eager to marry him and submit to it.

She didn't happen to be one of them, however. Not that it made any difference now, one way or the other ...

That afternoon she set out for the gorge. Mrs Adams, to her surprise, for she seemed such a practical, down-to-earth sort of woman, was sitting at a table on the back verandah engaged in making a beautiful and very detailed painting of a bunch of wildflowers. Farrell had sought her out to tell her where she was going when she discovered her painting, and apologised for the interruption.

'May I look? It's beautiful—you're very talented.'

'Talented? I'm painstaking,' the housekeeper corrected her with a slight smile. 'It's a sure way of filling in my spare time.'

'You must find it lonely here,' Farrell suggested.

'Not a bit. I've always lived in the bush—I wouldn't live anywhere else. Besides, I often have company. My husband comes home most weekends—Mr Sandfort may have mentioned to you that he's a building maintenance worker in Ansell. Then I have two small grandchildren who sometimes come to stay. My daughter lives in Roebourne.'

'And then there are Mr Sandfort's guests,' Farrell said after a second. It sounded like fishing and so it was, for she had thought of Helen, but it didn't get any results.

'That's right,' agreed Mrs Adams pleasantly, and quietly returned her attention to her painting, putting a definite end to the conversation.

Farrell grimaced a little and set off for the gorge, reflect-

ing that the housekeeper, as well as being a paragon as far as
running the house was concerned, was the epitome of dis-
cretion.

She didn't walk far up the gorge. It was very beautiful but more than a little awesome. It grew narrower and
narrower as she progressed. The towering rock walls closed
in and the path was almost impossible to follow through the
wattles and eucalypts and paperbarks, tangled as it was
with wildflowers and green ferns. It was obviously seldom
used, and probably known only to visitors to Quindalup. In
the deep green shadows to one side, Farrell could see pools
of still water, shadowed, secret and silent. An occasional
bird flew up against the blue of the sky, its wings flashing in
sunlight, and sometimes a lizard slithered away through
dry eucalyptus leaves and flaking bark, but otherwise it
was like moving through an uninhabited world.

Farrell spent two days swimming and walking and waiting, but Larry Sandfort didn't come, and she began to feel
jumpy with frustration. Not a single vehicle ever came
along the narrow bush road, and she and Mrs Adams were
locked away in a tiny world that held no one else. Then one
day while she was in the gorge she heard the drone of a
small plane and saw it flying overhead. Later in the evening, as she came moodily back to the bungalow, it was there
again, glinting tiny and silver against the azure sky.

In the bungalow garden, Mrs Adams was hunting the
fowls back into the yard, and Farrell asked her idly,
'What's going on up there?'

Mrs Adams didn't even look up. 'That's Mr Sandfort's
plane,' she said matter-of-factly.

Farrell's heart leapt. 'Is he coming here? Is—is there
somewhere to land?'

'Oh dear, no!' Mrs Adams exclaimed. 'He's mustering
sheep out at Mullamulla Downs, that's all. I wonder if he
brought Helen back from Perth with him?'

Helen! Lovely Helen! Before she could stop herself, Farrell had asked simply, 'Who's Helen?'

'My daughter-in-law,' said the other woman calmly.

Farrell's head spun. So Helen was married—Larry had lost her to another man. It occurred to her that Mrs Adams' son must be powerfully attractive for Helen to have preferred him to Larry. She stood watching the house-keeper shooing the hens across the garden as her mind tried to process what had been said. She hadn't known Larry was going to Perth, but now she realised that must be where he had gone to sign the papers he had mentioned. Why on earth, though, would he be likely to bring another man's wife back with him? And why was he mustering sheep from the air? Why, come to that, was he mustering sheep at all, when he was a mining man and not a pastoralist? It was amazing, she reflected, how many unexpected things there were to be discovered in another person's life. Who would ever suspect Mrs Adams of doing those fine, meticulous flower paintings, for instance? Or Larry Sandfort of read-ing poetry, or of mustering sheep?

Rather thoughtfully, she followed the housekeeper across the garden, and when all the hens were safely shut up inside their yard, she asked casually, 'Why is Mr Sandfort using his plane to work the sheep?'

'Oh well, Bob Nelson doesn't have a plane now, and they're shorthanded out there since the son's gone,' Mrs Adams said almost reluctantly, it seemed to Farrell. She glanced at the large rather mannish watch she wore as she spoke, and immediately set off back to the house.

Farrell gave up and let her go. She had already observed that Mrs Adams had set a strict routine for herself which she followed scrupulously every day. In her life, every moment was accounted for, and now, no doubt, it was time to peel the vegetables or make the dessert or switch on the radio, or goodness knew what. Farrell would have liked to ask her some more questions, whether it sounded like prying or not—such as who was Bob Nelson, and where had his son gone, and what was Mullamulla Downs to Larry Sandfort, but she couldn't bring herself to follow the other woman to the kitchen.

Now, more than ever, she wished irritably that Larry Sandfort would come back to Quindalup and—and let her out of this cage she was in—though heaven knew where she would fly to!

'He could have taken me to Perth,' she thought resentfully. But he hadn't given her the choice, and she wasn't altogether sure that she would have gone.

CHAPTER SIX

ON Saturday afternoon, Mrs Adams' husband Jim came home. Farrell, hearing the car, thought it was Larry. She was in the garden behind the house reading a novel in which she had somehow managed to work up a bit of interest, and she tossed it down abruptly. Her first impulse was to jump to her feet and hurry round to the drive, but she restrained herself. Let Larry come and find her! She didn't want him to imagine she was delighted to see him. She wondered if Helen, Mrs Adams' daughter-in-law, would be with him, and somehow she hoped not. She didn't feel like—coping with lovely Helen.

When, some five minutes later, it was a rather wiry man with a pointed beard and eyes crinkled with laughter who appeared instead of Larry, she couldn't believe it. She stared at him with such a stunned expression on her face that he said with a smile, 'It's all right—I'm only Jim Adams. You're Miss Fitzgerald, aren't you? I've brought you some mail from town—two letters.'

Two letters! One would be from her father, of course. Could the other be from Larry, explaining his non-arrival at Quindalup? Farrell took the letters eagerly, and managed to collect herself sufficiently to murmur something conventional and polite when Jim Adams asked was she enjoying her holiday.

'I'm here to make sure the pumps are behaving properly,' he told her, 'and to replenish the larder with a bit of fresh meat and a few groceries my wife asked me to bring.'

Farrell nodded, scanning the two envelopes and discovering with a feeling of disappointment that the second letter was from her aunt. Well, why should she expect Larry Sandfort to bother with apologies to her? He had probably put her completely out of his mind. Farrell decided she didn't like the way he was treating her—not one little bit. In fact, what with one thing and another, she was beginning quite positively to hate him. She wanted nothing so much as to get away from his famous Quindalup, and if she could do so before he turned up—if he ever *did* turn up!—then so much the better.

As Jim Adams walked away, an obvious and brilliant idea came into her head. Of course! She would go with him when he went back to town! She would insist. And, just in case Larry had left any *instructions* about her, she wouldn't ask, she'd simply present herself and her luggage the moment he showed signs of leaving, which would probably be some time tomorrow afternoon or night. She would pack after dinner tonight.

That settled, and considerably heartened by the thought of action, Farrell gave her attention to her mail. She read her father's letter first, anxious to discover what his reaction to her news about her movements had been.

He was, it appeared, quite happy—even delighted—to learn she was under Larry Sandfort's protection. 'What a piece of luck, darling, to have such a man take an interest in you! I've often felt guilty about my own inability to provide you with a normal family home, and it disturbed me when you decided to leave Perth—and, to be truthful, even more when you left here, recently. But I realise that neither Jean nor I have the right to prevent you from going your own way about finding a meaningful life for yourself. Is there any chance of getting yourself some position with Ansell-Sandfort Mining? In the Perth offices, I mean—I wouldn't like to see you working in Ansell. I had a very nice letter from your protector by the way, and I feel reassured you'll be completely safe doing your meditating at

Quindalup. Between you and me, I had the feeling when he was here asking for you—he'll have told you about that—that he was more than a little interested in you. It's quite an amazing coincidence you should have run into each other, isn't it? Well, darling, I enclose a cheque and hope to hear more news soon. Your loving Father.'

Farrell finished reading the letter and folded it up again thoughtfully. So Larry had written to her father, had he?—and obviously her father had hopes of a romance developing between them. Well, that was about the most unlikely thing in the world to happen. Things had changed quite drastically since she and Larry had so strangely run into each other again!

Her aunt's letter was a brief one and had been forwarded on from the Coral Reef Hotel. Its main import was that Jean had succeeded in having Farrell's course deferred till next year. She was quite sure her niece's unrest was no more than the aftermath of that attack of illness she'd had, and she assured her that she would be welcome to come back to Perth at any time. 'The academic life is a very satisfying one, Farrell. It would be a pity for you to reject it because of post-'flu depression.' She was Farrell's 'affectionate aunt, Jean Roseblade.'

It was a pleasant letter, but it was entirely unemotional, and Farrell was sadly aware that warmth was one of the main things that had been lacking in her life in Perth.

That night after dinner, she went to her bedroom and busily packed her bags, leaving out only the necessities for the following day. On Monday, she decided, she would cash her father's cheque in Ansell, and then somehow or other she would get herself on to the plane, even if it meant using an asumed name and disguising herself with scarf and sunglasses! Her protector, when he returned from Mulla-mulla Downs, would find the bird had flown.

Farrell's plans, however, went sadly awry.

She broke her routine on Sunday—no morning swim, no afternoon walk—because she wasn't going to miss that lift in Jim Adams' car for anything on earth. The day seemed endless, the heat interminable, and when dinner went by and he still had shown no signs of departing, she began to feel nervily tensed up. Surely he must go soon, she thought, sitting in the dark on the verandah, her ears alert, her luggage by the steps. But the moon moved slowly, inexorably, across the garden and nothing happened. Farrell waited and waited, until through sheer weariness, she fell asleep.

She woke with a start to find it was after one o'clock, and she almost wept. She must have missed hearing the car! But a stumbling walk across the garden revealed that the car was still there, and with an inward prayer of thanks, she went wearily to bed. She was awake well before six—but this time she was too late, as she discovered when she had flung herself into some clothes and hurried outside. She was so frustrated and so furious she opened her cases and scattered the contents all over the room. Aunt Jean would have disapproved thoroughly. Farrell remembered throwing things about like that when she was in a temper soon after she went to Perth, but she had never done such a thing since. It had been trained out of her with several other traits that her aunt regarded as undesirably emotional or exhibitionist. Well, it was all flooding back now...

She lost heart that day, and she thought moodily that she really *hated* Larry Sandfort—for dumping her, deserting her, forgetting her. She never wanted to see him again except to acquaint him of just that fact. And of course, he wouldn't care. She was lounging listlessly on the verandah that afternoon wearing a sleeveless top that showed her midriff, and a long cotton skirt, when she saw Mrs Adams come briskly along the path from the back of the house. She looked smart in a blue linen dress, and she carried a handbag and a flat parcel. Farrell was on her feet in a flash.

If the housekeeper was going to Ansell—and where else was there to go?—then she was going too. She felt a momentary dismay at the thought of her belongings still scattered in confusion about her room, but she dismissed it, and leaping down from the verandah, she raced across the garden towards the garages with their screen of bougainvillea.

Mrs Adams was just settling herself behind the steering wheel.

'Are you going to Ansell, Mrs Adams?'

'That's right. I'm taking some paintings to the craft shop, and then I have a few purchases to make. Was there something you wanted, Miss Fitzgerald?' She glanced at her watch as she spoke, and Farrell thought wryly, oh yes, she'd have her movements worked out to the last split second. Well, today she would have to make a few adjustments.

She said imperiously, 'Yes, I want to come with you. It's urgent I should get to the bank,' she improvised. 'If you'd told me you were going, I'd have been ready. You'll have to wait a few minutes.'

She didn't wait for an answer but hurried back to the house. She needed shoes—she was barefoot—her handbag and her cheque. Apart from that, she didn't dare take any longer than was needed to thrust pyjamas, toilet things, and a random armful of clothes into her big folding beach bag before she darted back to the car. One never knew—Mrs Adams just might have taken off without her, particularly if Larry had said she was not to leave, which Farrell wouldn't put it past him to do.

The housekeeper drove fast and expertly, without wasting time or energy in making conversation. If she wondered what Farrell had in her beach bag, she didn't ask. In Ansell, she let Farrell out at the shopping complex, after arranging to pick her up at the same place at five-thirty. Farrell had no intention of going back to Quindalup, but she nodded agreement, and thought ruefully that she would have to live without her belongings till she found somewhere they could be sent on to her.

She went straight to the bank and cashed her cheque, then debated whether she should ring the air services or present herself in person. Without flattering herself, she rather thought she might manage to be more persuasive in person, and anyhow she needn't give her name, and they wouldn't know what Farrell Fitzgerald looked like, surely! She managed to get herself a taxi, and soon she was speeding out of town to the small airfield. She felt full of nervous excitement. She had absolutely no plans, and at the moment she didn't care where the next plane went to so long as she could be on it. She would show Larry Sandfort he couldn't treat her this way any longer! She had seen his small plane in the air again that morning, so it was reasonably safe to conclude he was still at Mullamulla Downs, which was reassuring, and meant that she wouldn't be likely to encounter him at the hotel if she had to stay there overnight.

At the rather desolate iron-coloured airfield, she asked the taxi driver to wait and walked over to the administration building, which was little more than a shed. There were several small planes on the ground, but no sign of activity at the moment. In the shade of a big poinciana tree was a dusty four-wheel-drive vehicle that Farrell recognised with a slight shock as belonging to Larry. No doubt he would pick it up there when he came in from Mullamulla Downs.

When she walked into the booking office, the young man at the desk looked at her interestedly and smiled pleasantly as he asked what he could do for her. Farrell smiled back engagingly.

'I wanted some information about the next flight to—to Port Hedland. There's nothing this afternoon, I suppose.'

'No. Eleven-thirty tomorrow,' he told her. She noticed

uneasily that he was scrutinising her pretty thoroughly, his gaze lingering on her curly hair, and she wished that she had covered it with a head scarf—only she had collected her things so haphazardly she doubted whether she had one. Still, she could have bought something. Now it looked as if it might be too late, because in her heart she knew what he was going to tell her before he said another word.

'I'm afraid that plane's booked out. We have a lot of to-ing and fro-ing going on at the moment, I really can't give you anything. Best thing for you to do will be to keep trying, day by day.' He smiled as he said it, but Farrell was totally incapable of smiling back at him. She felt almost as much infuriated by him as she was by Larry Sandfort, and without a word she turned on her heel and went outside.

What did she do next? Because she wasn't going to meet Mrs Adams at five-thirty and be taken quietly back to Quindalup. So she stayed at the hotel. Indefinitely. Until she won. Because surely even Larry Sandfort wouldn't drag her screaming to his car! Oh God, what a country to be stranded in! And what a man to have drawn as a protector!

As she walked moodily in the direction of the waitng taxi, she heard the drone of a plane overhead, and shading her eyes against the glare, she watched it coming in to the airstrip. She had a feeling it was Larry Sandfort's plane, and a moment later she asked the taxi driver, 'Whose is that plane, coming in?'

'Larry Sandfort's,' he said promptly. 'Been out muster-ing on Mullamulla Downs, I hear. Don't know what's bringing him in to town today.'

Farrell stood for a moment, her hand on the taxi door, debating what to do. It looked as though she was going to have to see him, whether she chose to or not. Even if he went out to Quindalup to see her, he'd still be coming back to town after that—and she, as he would very well know, would still be there. It might as well happen now as later.

She discovered her jaw was tightly clenched. How she hated him!—for his power in being able to make a prisoner of her for no good reason at all. *That* was something that had to stop.

She told the taxi driver, 'I'll wait here and come into town with Mr Sandfort. How much do I owe you?'

He told her, looking slightly startled, then handed out her beach bag as she got some money out of her purse. As he drove off, she walked across to Larry's Landrover and waited near it, in the shade. He brought his plane in, and presently she saw him leave it and stroll across to the administration building and disappear inside. She had kept herself discreetly in the shadow of the poinciana tree, but he hadn't even glanced that way. Eventually he reappeared, and when he was close enough, she stepped into view.

She had expected him to be surprised and even angry, but he gave no signs of being either. And that, she thought with a feeling of irritation, was probably because his—his *spies* had just told him she'd been trying only five minutes ago to book herself on to a flight out of the area. For all she knew, he might even have been told she'd dismissed her taxi and was waiting for him. Anything was possible where Larry Sandfort was concerned.

He wore blue denim pants and jacket, and the bleached streaks in his thick hair gleamed in the sun. She watched him come closer and closer, with a reluctant fascination. His step was so damnably assured, and she hadn't remembered his shoulders were so broad. And his eyes—his eyes were so blue they scorched like blue fire, right through to her very soul. Farrell felt a tremor go through her. Somehow, his reality was totally different from the image she'd been nurturing in her mind. Her confidence in herself slipped sideways.

'You waited for me,' he said, and her eyes traced the curve of his lips as he spoke, then returned to the enigma of his eyes. 'Quite a homecoming! Get in, Farrell.' He hadn't locked the door and he swung it open for her with a flourish.

She had no idea what to say, and simply got into the seat with her beach bag, and in a moment Larry was beside her. She could have been a wife waiting for her husband to come back from a business trip or from work, and now, ridiculously, as they left the airfield, she wanted to ask him, 'How did the muster go?' Instead, she said disagreeably, 'Why won't you let me out of this place?'

'That's the sixty-four-dollar question,' he said. 'Why won't I? I tell myself it's out of an altruistic concern for you—but I'm not at all sure about that, Farrell. I expected to see you in town today, by the way. That's why I'm here. A bright girl like you wouldn't miss out on a trip into Ansell . . . Have you been making the most of Quindalup?'

'I—I *hate* it,' she said. It wasn't true, but she hoped it hurt him. 'There's not a thing to do there, and I'm not going back.' Her voice wavered uncertainly on the last words. She had been so positive she was not going back, that he couldn't force her. Now, she was not sure at all. If he chose, he could take her straight out to Quindalup now, and she supposed fatalistically that that was exactly what he would do.

He said pleasantly, 'I'd have thought you'd be a lot happier there than in Ansell.'

'With nothing to do? With no one to talk to?' she said querulously. 'That housekeeper of yours is no company— she has every minute of the day accounted for. I might as well be alone. I'm like a bird in a cage. Just don't—don't take me back there.'

She saw his brows rise. 'We're heading for Ansell, Farrell. We'll talk about it,' he added slowly. 'You must have had a few ideas about your future while you've been fretting in your cage. I can't believe you've been doing quite that, by the way. You're more tanned than you were last time we met. Have you been exploring the gorge?'

'Exploring!' she repeated scornfully. 'Don't try to humour me, as if I were a child! You—you dumped me out there, yet you—you go on about other people deserting me.'

'I didn't desert you, Farrell, and you know it,' he said curtly. 'And I certainly didn't compromise you, make you my mistress—and then leave you.'

Farrell coloured angrily. How he did like to take it for granted that she and Mark had been lovers! Well, why should she try to argue her innocence with him? He wasn't likely to believe her, and anyhow, she no longer cared what he thought. All she wanted was to get away from him and from here.

They had reached Ansell by now, and he glanced at his watch.

'Mrs Adams will be leaving for Quindalup in a few minutes,' he remarked.

'*I'm* not going back to Quindalup,' Farrell said quickly.

'Did you tell my housekeeper that?' he asked dryly as he drove slowly along the tree-lined street.

She hated herself for feeling guilty and dishonest. 'No, I didn't. It happens to be my own business.'

'So you were just going to let her wait for you—and not turn up.'

'Of course I wasn't. I—I intended to meet her and let her know.'

'I see.' He didn't sound as if he believed her, and to tell the truth Farrell was not clear in her mind just what she had intended. If she'd been able to take off in a plane this afternoon, she'd have done so without a qualm, and left Mrs Adams high and dry. Yet she hadn't really believed she'd get a seat on the plane today—or on tomorrow's flight either, come to that. She had known in her heart that Larry Sandfort wouldn't let her escape as easily as all that.

'Well, where's the meeting place?' he wanted to know.

'At the shopping complex. But don't think I'm——'

'All right, all right, you want to press the point that you're not prepared to go back to Quindalup ... Have you left your luggage somewhere?'

'No. I—I didn't have time to get packed up. I didn't know Mrs Adams was coming to town.'

He made no comment on that, and presently pulled up near the shopping complex. Mrs Adams was already there, and Farrell and Larry both got out of the Landrover and walked along to her car.

'Hello, Mrs Adams. How are things? I hope you haven't been kept waiting. I'm afraid Miss Fitzgerald won't be going back with you in any case—she's staying in Ansell to have dinner with me.'

Mrs Adams smiled pleasantly, said that that would be nice and thanked Mr Sandfort for the information, then without further ado got her car moving.

When she had gone, Farrell said emphatically, 'I don't want to have dinner with you, Mr Sandfort. All I want is to be able to take the plane to Port Hedland tomorrow.'

He looked at her intently, his blue eyes narrowed. 'So you've made plans around Port Hedland, have you? Well, you must have dinner somewhere, Farrell, so you might as well have it with me, and you can tell me all about it.'

Farrell grimaced and gave in. There wasn't anything to tell him, but maybe by the time she had to explain herself she would have thought of something plausible, though at the moment her mind was a complete blank—and so, it seemed, was her future. She began to have an uncomfortable feeling that she would finish up back in Perth with Aunt Jean.

'Get in, Farrell,' said Larry, opening the door of the Landrover.

Farrell got in.

'I'll get my key and see if there are any messages for me,' Larry told Farrell when they reached the motel. She was carrying her beach bag and wishing futilely that she had managed to bring all her luggage with her. It would make things so much easier. 'You can have a brush-up in my suite.'

'No, thank you,' she said, colouring furiously. 'I—I'll take a room here for the night.'

'I very much doubt whether you'll get accommodation. There's a coach full of tourists here and as well as that we have several official visitors in Ansell. I can practically promise you there are no vacancies.'

Farrell wasn't prepared to accept that. 'I'll find out for myself, Mr Sandfort.'

He raised his eyebrows. 'Go ahead, then.' He turned his back on her and moved towards the desk, and she brushed past him quickly, determined to get in ahead of him, in case he had ideas of issuing instructions that she was to be told the motel was full.

To her chagrin, he was right. There were no vacancies, and of course there was no other hotel in Ansell. He certainly had it all his own way! So what on earth did she do now? She waited helplessly while he exchanged pleasantries with the girl on duty, and told her as she handed him his key and a bundle of letters, 'I'll make arrangements for Miss Fitzgerald here—there'll be no worries.' He tossed his key casually into the air and caught it, and as casually said to Farrell, 'Come along now.'

Farrell felt trapped. She was getting used to feeling that way. She wondered what arrangements he had it in mind to make for her, and as far as she could see there were just two alternatives. One was that she should stay here in his suite, which she quite definitely was not going to do. The other was that he should take her back to Quindalup. She wasn't prepared to do that either, without first exacting a promise from him that he would let her leave town on the plane tomorrow. Unfortunately, she was hardly in a position to bargain. She was, in fact—as usual—at his mercy. The very thought made her feel tired.

'Do you want to take a shower?' he asked her when they reached his suite.

'No, thank you,' she said distantly. 'A—a wash is all I need.'

One corner of his mouth quirked up. 'Don't read too much into my enquiry. I was merely being polite in offering you first option ... Do you have a change of clothing, by the way?' His eyes skimmed over her abbreviated top, her long skirt, then went thoughtfully to her bulging beach bag.

Farrell made a frantic effort to think what she had stuffed into that beach bag when she had gathered up a hasty armful of clothes, but she had no idea. Nevertheless, she told him coolly, 'I have everything I need.'

'Well, change your blouse,' he suggested. 'The skirt will do.'

'Thank you,' she said sarcastically.

He moved towards one of the doors that opened off the suite, and opened it. 'Make yourself at home in here,' he offered.

A little suspiciously, Farrell looked inside the door and discovered a small attractive room furnished with a divan, a couple of armchairs, and a chest over which was a big mirror. A further door led into a washroom.

'Take your time,' said Larry. 'Pour yourself a drink when you're ready, if you feel like it.' The look in his eyes suggested she looked as if she needed something to buck her up. 'There's plenty of your favourite tipple—gin and tonic, isn't it? I'll join you presently.'

'Don't hurry on my account,' Farrell said. But she said it beneath her breath as he turned away.

She waited till she heard the click of his bedroom door

before she went back to fetch her beach bag, and then she
locked herself into the small room and used the washroom,
discovering fresh towels and soap there. Her skirt had a
black background with a pattern of small flowers on it, and
luckily she had scooped up a black blouse—a slinky one
with long sleeves and a bateau neckline. She changed into it
and looked at herself critically in the mirror, and decided
she didn't look bad. The red sandals she had on were pass-
able for evening wear, too. Not that she cared what she
looked like really, she told herself.

She gave her hair a thorough brushing and made up her
face lightly, taking her time about it, so that she was surprised when there was a knock at the door and Larry called,
'Are you coming to join me in a drink, Farrell?'

She made a grimace, then shrugged at her reflection and
tried a smile. Life was certainly strange lately! When she'd
left Aunt Jean's it had never entered her head that in a few
weeks' time she'd have been through a number of experiences totally unrelated to the life she'd lived in Perth. She'd
imagined she'd be 'home' with her father and her stepmother—safe and loved, with plenty of time to decide what
she was going to do now she'd abandoned the idea of
following in her aunt's footsteps. Instead, she had been far
from safe, and at this very moment she didn't really know if
she was safe or not . . .

She unlocked the door almost expecting to find Larry
waiting for her in his dressing gown—he surely couldn't
have showered and dressed in so short a time. But he had,
and by now he was standing at the cocktail cabinet, his back
towards her. He wore a white shirt and charcoal grey light-
weight pants, and his hair was dark from the shower. He
turned when he heard her move across the floor, and his
gaze flicked over her before his blue eyes looked directly
into hers. It did curious things to her and she didn't know
why. It was perhaps just that he seemed to look at her in a

different way. He thought she looked good—she could see it there unconcealed in his eyes, and it made her unaccountably nervous. Because wasn't it supposed to give you confidence if you knew someone approved of your appearance?

She seated herself and more to conceal her attack of nerves than for any other reason told him argumentatively, 'Gin and tonic's not my favourite tipple, if that's why you're planning to give me. I—I'd sooner have a small dry sherry.'

He smiled slightly. 'Right—you may have whatever you like. There's some cheese and a few olives in the refrigerator if you'd care to fetch them.'

Farrell felt him watching her as she crossed the room, and she wished she knew what went on in his head, but there was no hope of *that*. She opened the refrigerator and found small cubes of cheese in a covered container, green olives in another. Self-consciously she placed them on the low coffee table and sat down again, not even raising her eyes when he handed her a small glass of sherry. Disconcertingly, she recalled what Cecile had said to her father that day at the Coral Reef Hotel—'He's the kind of man who starts making love to you at the dinner table'. Well, they weren't at the dinner table, but they were very much alone. And he had once asked her to marry him. That seemed so incredible now that without meaning to, she looked up and caught him looking back at her, a totally baffling expression on his face.

She sipped her sherry, took one of the olives, and said jerkily, 'I had a letter from my father. Did he—did he write to you too?'

'I suppose he may have,' he said absently. 'I haven't looked through my mail yet. It can wait—so long as you can assure me your father's not likely to be uttering dire threats of revenge unless I free his daughter from the cage I've shut her in.'

He spoke half humorously, but Farrell refused to smile. Not for anything would she have told Larry Sandfort that her father seemed actually pleased he was taking an interest in her, and even had ideas in his head that there could be a romance in the air. She would make sure, when she wrote back, that she disillusioned him on *that* point . . .

'Oh no, you really fooled him,' she told Larry, and had the satisfaction of seeing an expression of annoyance cross his face.

'And what do you mean by that?'

'Just that I think you're behaving very badly. You—you're keeping me here against my will. And if you don't see that I'm able to get a seat on the plane tomorrow, Mr Sandfort,' she added, warming to her theme, 'then I shall write to my father and tell him the truth.'

His eyes narrowed. 'I don't quite know what you mean by the truth . . . But I'll write to your father too, Farrell—and tell him that when I found you, you were with a man. Your stepmother will back up the truth of that, no doubt.'

'You're not—fair,' she said angrily, though she knew that once again she was defeated. Yet why was he so intent on keeping her here, now he no longer wanted to marry her? 'What do you *want* of me?' she demanded, raising her head to look at him challengingly.

He appeared to consider her question, staring at his glass of Scotch while he did so. Finally he said enigmatically, 'I don't know that I want anything of you, Farrell. I just haven't made up my mind what's to be done about you. A short time ago, I'd have been in no doubt. As it is, I haven't yet come to terms with the situation. But it won't do you any harm to cool your heels while I come to a decision.'

'Then I wish you'd hurry up.' Farrell, who wasn't at all sure what he meant, felt herself smouldering. The arrogance of him—taking her over like this, holding her helpless in this tiny oasis of a town, isolated in the wild ranges!

Possibly there were other places in the world where a girl could be more helpless, but to Farrell, who had never been out of Western Australia, this was the ultimate. She had done herself not one whit of good in managing to get away from Quindalup. She might just as well have stayed there and submitted to her fate. At least that way she would have been spared a little more of his company!

CHAPTER SEVEN

FARRELL was very cool over dinner. She'd had plenty of training in being cool and detached in Perth, but she found it didn't come so easily now. It needed a decided effort. She was thankful anyhow that he didn't make too much of a thing about what she planned to do once she reached Port Hedland.

'Just look for work,' she told him indifferently when he asked, and he let it go at that.

'What about the writing? Have you tried your hand out there lately? You must have accumulated a few experiences you need to work out of your system, lately. That's said to make good material, I believe.'

Farrell looked at him stonily. 'I've been too frustrated at Quindalup to settle down to anything.'

'That's a pity. You might have found it helpful, even therapeutic. I'd have imagined it a good environment for creativity. I know Mrs Adams finds it so. Did you have a look at some of her flower paintings?'

'Yes. They're very beautiful. But it's different for her. She lives there—she's married—she's got everything worked out.'

'No one has everything worked out, Farrell. And believe me, life hasn't been all that easy for Lesley Adams.' His blue eyes darkened and he looked at her sombrely across the table. 'I don't suppose she's told you much about her life.'

'Not much,' Farrell agreed. 'She's always so busy we've hardly exchanged two words. Not that she isn't very pleasant and agreeable,' she added hastily. 'She is.'

'Yes. Well, being busy in various ways probably serves a

119

purpose. Mrs Adams lost her only son in a plane accident about a year ago.'

'Oh—I'm sorry,' Farrell exclaimed. 'I knew she had a married son, but I didn't know he——' Her voice faltered and trailed off. Her *only* son, Larry had said. *That* meant that Helen was a widow, which surely explained Larry's loving birthday card, and also the fact that Mrs Adams expected him to bring Helen up here from Perth. But if he was interested in Helen, why had he asked her, Farrell, to marry him, so short a time ago? She wouldn't have thought him to be the kind of man who acted on impulse—and he had gone back for her, as he had promised he would. She simply couldn't understand him at all.

She was staring at him, her eyes wide. 'What—what happened?' she heard herself ask huskily.

'He was out at Mullamulla Downs and he and my manager's son took the plane up. They flew it too low and crashed into some trees. The plane went up in smoke and young Adams lost his life.' He was silent for a moment, his blue eyes sombre. 'Bob Nelson prefers to muster from the ground these days. He hasn't invested in another plane.'

Listening thoughtfully, Farrell found she now had the answer to some of the questions she hadn't asked Mrs Adams. Mullamulla Downs must be Larry's property, and Bob Nelson was his manager. As for the son who had gone——

'Was his—son injured?' she asked quietly.

He nodded. 'But not badly. He got over it.'

He said no more until Farrell asked, 'Is Mullamulla Downs your sheep station, Larry?'

'Yes. I inherited it from my father. But as you know, I've made my career in mining so I've put in a manager. However, I'm not the complete absentee landlord. I spend a fair bit of time on the property, and when I can put in the time, I do a bit of mustering from the air. It's a big run, and using a plane means you can get the sheep on the move from the most remote paddocks and bring them in for the station hands to take over. I won't pretend I do it merely from a sense of duty—it's work I enjoy.'

Farrell felt a curious stirring. She thought it would have been a great deal more interesting to have gone to Mullamulla Downs with Larry than to have been dropped off at Quindalup and stranded there. But perhaps Helen was at Mullamulla Downs—waiting now for him to come back.

Disconcerted by her thoughts, she finished her dinner and laid down her knife and fork.

'Dessert?' he asked.

'No, thank you. I'd just like some coffee.'

He ordered coffee for two, then took up the conversation where they had left it.

'Unfortunately for my father, I was an only child. My mother didn't live long enough to bear other children. Life in the North-West's hard for a woman, and in those days we were more isolated than now, and very short of comforts. My father believed in adapting to the environment rather than altering it to suit his needs,' he added dryly, 'and he stuck to his own rather spartan ways until the day he died.' He paused while the waitress brought the coffee, and Farrell reflected that she must seem a very soft and pampered creature to someone like Larry Sandfort. All that fuss she had made about being dumped at Quindalup——She was beginning to realise there was a great deal about this man that she didn't know, and to feel a vague regret that the crash course at Quindalup had never eventuated.

The taped background music that had been playing softly while they were eating had now been turned up slightly, and the lights had been equally lowered, and two or three couples moved on to the tiny parquet floor. Farrell turned back from glancing at them to give some attention to her coffee and to say to Larry Sandfort, 'Go on—please tell me some more.'

He raised his eyebrows. 'Are you interested?' She nodded, flushing a little, and he resumed. 'Well, let's see—we had no electric light—no electricity plant. Our house was lit by kerosene lamps, and most of the cooking was done in camp ovens. We grew our own vegetables—our water came from a creek-bed soak. As far as station management was concerned, my father was a perfectionist, and he never overstocked, which meant the land was kept in good condition, and the feed was never eaten out. One thing we did have, by the way, was a strip where the flying doctor could land if he was needed, and my mother made her last journey by plane. Well, I've made improvements at the homestead since my father died—Bob and Muriel Nelson are as comfortable as anyone else out here.' His lips curved sardonically. 'Of course, it's a necessary inducement to stay ... Now, Farrell—finish your coffee, because I'm going to ask you to dance. You might as well make the most of your release from solitary confinement.'

Farrell felt faintly alarmed, for some reason, and her instinct was to say no, she didn't want to dance with him. She glanced uneasily at the few couples locked together, scarcely moving, on the softly lit dance floor. Her lips parted, yet she didn't refuse him as she had intended to do. Instead, she finished her coffee obediently, and a few seconds later they had joined the others on the tiny circle of parquet flooring.

Larry held her to him in a close embrace, exactly the way every other male was holding his partner, and she had no worries about following his lead, because there were no steps to follow. They stood together, their thighs touching, his cheek against her hair, as they rocked infinitesimally and rhythmically to the soft music. Soon Farrell was aware that her nearness affected him physically. He was probably a very sexy man, she thought, tensing slightly. Much more so than Mark. Sexier—and more experienced. So what? That was no reason why her breath should be growing uneven and more uneven. He was doing no more than—dance with her. She made an effort to relax, to study sensibly her own reaction to his closeness. That other time when she had cut her finger and he had put his mouth on it—she had panicked then, quite stupidly. She wasn't going to tear herself away in a fright this time, she'd be quite sane, quite analytical—she'd be a credit to Aunt Jean's unemotional training . . .

She managed it just long enough to discover that something both pleasurable and painful was happening in her own body—that she was becoming more and more tantalisingly aware of Larry's physical being. It was not just the hardness of his thighs against hers, or the feel of his chest against her bosom. As well, it was his cheek against her hair, the heavy warmth of his hand on her back, that burned through the silky black stuff of her shirt. It was the way he was twisting the fingers of his left hand with those of her right hand, so that excitement raced through her every nerve.

Certainly Farrell Fitzgerald was not entirely cold and unresponsive! Or did it all ultimately depend on how far he went? Here in the restaurant she knew she was perfectly safe—that nothing more was going to be asked of her——

She raised her face, and the emotion that shot through her as she encountered his blue eyes looking back deeply into hers was penetrating and inexplicable. She felt herself go limp, felt moisture on the palms of her hands. A long moment passed and then he deftly turned her away from him, and with one hand under her elbow, guided her back to the table. She felt a mixture of relief and disappointment as she tilted her head a little and smiled and said briefly and falsely, 'That was nice . . . By the way, would it be too much to ask what arrangements you've made about me for tonight?'

'Not at all. I'm taking you back to Quindalup. So if you'll collect your handbag, we'll go now.'

'Oh,' said Farrell, briefly and inadequately. She bit her lip nervously. She had made such a to-do before about not going back to Quindalup, yet what alternative was there? It was the obvious solution for tonight, since there were no vacancies at the hotel, and she certainly wouldn't be interested in sharing Larry's suite! Besides, she still had her luggage to collect.

She picked up her small handbag and without further comment, crossed the room with him to the exit. She was conscious for the first time that a number of people were taking an interest in their movements—and had probably, earlier, been interested in their dining—and dancing—together. After all, Larry Sandfort was a big shot in this mining town, and so far he was unmarried. She supposed there was possibly some curious speculating going on about her and Helen Adams, and the thought caused her to experience a feeling of distaste. She wondered, as they made their way to his suite, whether he would stay at Quindalup for the night or return to Mullamulla Downs and, possibly, the lovely Helen.

She ached to know, but she didn't ask him.

She fell asleep in the car on the way to Quindalup, and woke to find herself slumped against him, her head resting on his shoulder. She drew away quickly, yawning, shivering slightly, and looking out at the black loneliness of the night.

'Are we nearly there?'

'Sure. Round the next curve in the road you'll see the lights of the house.'

'What time is it?'

'It's early—not yet ten o'clock.'

Farrell had edged a little away from him, and glanced now at his profile, barely discernible in the darkness, remote, unreadable. Yet fascinating despite everything. Suddenly she had to ask him.

'Are you—going back to town tonight after you've unloaded me?'

'Into your cell, you mean?' She heard faint amusement in his voice. 'No, I'm not going back. I'll stay awhile.'

Her heart leaped inexplicably. 'Well, aren't I lucky!' she said sarcastically. 'When did you decide on that? You must be feeling like a holiday this time.'

'Perhaps I am,' he agreed.

In another couple of minutes she saw the lights, yellow and soft and very small in the immensity of the darkness and silence. She wondered if Mrs Adams would be waiting up. It was her usual habit to go to bed at nine-thirty each night, but perhaps Larry had already told her he would be coming to stay, perhaps he had planned it well ahead, and it had nothing to do with Farrell Fitzgerald. Perhaps Mrs Adams would make them coffee, give them supper—a thing she never had done when Farrell was there on her own. If Farrell had wanted a bedtime snack, she was free to get it from the kitchen for herself. Tonight, everything was going to be different.

Her thoughts strayed back to those minutes she had spent in Larry's arms at the hotel—to her own very definite and quite unexpected response to the close physical contact with him. What could he have taught her about love—about passion—if she had come here with him as he had planned—without the episode with Mark to upset the applecart? She had the decided feeling he could have taught her a lot, that she would very quickly have recovered from her nervous puritanism. Now, she didn't think he wanted to teach her anything. He was convinced, of course, that she had already learned a good deal from someone else—from Mark Smith. Plenty of men these days would accept that without batting an eyelid—girls were liberated, they were as free to indulge in sex as men were, they weren't expected to be virgin brides. Larry obviously expected innocence in the girl he loved, and though Farrell was innocent, he probably wouldn't believe her if she tried to protest it now. She was well aware how guilty she had looked when she had admitted to sharing a room with Mark.

Didn't he mind, she wondered, her thoughts going off at a tangent, that Helen Adams was no longer innocent? Or—or *did* he mind? Was that the whole point? Was that why he had turned to her, Farrell—and, since, been disillusioned?

Her thoughts broke off as he pulled up outside the bungalow, and she suddenly felt both excited and afraid. This time, he was staying at Quindalup, and she knew that she couldn't go back to hating him as she had done when she was here on her own.

No, she didn't hate Larry Sandfort. But neither was she in love with him. Definitely not . . .

He reached for her beach bag as she stumbled out of the car and climbed the steps. The verandah light was on, but evidently Mrs Adams had retired, for she didn't appear to welcome them. Farrell stood blinking in the light, running her fingers through her curling hair, and as Larry joined her, she remarked nervily, 'You didn't bring a suitcase with you——'

'I don't need one. I keep a supply of my gear here.' He pushed open the door and flicked on an inside light, then followed her indoors. Farrell turned to take her bag and their fingers touched. She looked up quickly and caught a quizzical expression on his face.

'I—I think I'll go to bed,' she stammered.

'Straight away? It's not late,' he said mockingly.

'I know, but what else is there to do?' Colour surged into her face the minute she had said it, and she felt annoyed with herself.

'We can play some music, talk, make ourselves some supper.' He sounded amused, but she didn't look at him, so she didn't know if he was smiling or not. 'We'll take a walk down by the water, if you like. It's a beautiful night.'

Her heart thumped. She began to move down the hallway towards her bedroom and he followed her, and stood in the doorway as she switched on the light and deposited her bag on a chair. The room looked a complete mess with her clothes scattered around where she had thrown them in a fit of temper this morning. Only this morning! She hadn't cared what sort of havoc she created then, but now she felt embarrassed about her behaviour.

'Looks like a hurricane's hit the place,' commented Larry, his brows lifting. He looked at her curiously. 'Do you generally leave things like that?'

'No, of course not. I—I left in a hurry.' That of course didn't explain how the room had got into such disorder, but she didn't fill out her statement.

'You're untidy,' he remarked. 'I wouldn't have guessed it.' He leaned indolently against the door frame and watched her as, both angry and embarrassed, she stooped to gather up an armful of clothes that were tumbling from a chair on to the floor. Thrusting them into a drawer, she dropped a pair of panties and was further embarrassed when he picked them up and handed them to her. He did it as casually as if it had been a handkerchief, but that didn't stop her from turning scarlet.

His gaze wandered thoughtfully round the room. 'Well, I guess you'll be able to crawl into bed without staying up all night to set yourself to rights ... I'm going to make some coffee. If you want any, come and join me.'

Farrell didn't answer. She felt oddly put out at having him discover the mess she had left her room in. She wasn't really untidy, and it would give him just one more wrong idea about her. When she had lived with Aunt Jean, she had been a model of orderliness——— 'Your person and your possessions must be as orderly as your mind,' Aunt Jean had ordained. At her father's hotel, Farrell hadn't been quite so particular, but she had never been as disorganised as this. Larry had disappeared to the kitchen without waiting to know if she meant to join him or not, and she supposed he was probably disgusted with her. She wouldn't join him, she decided. It was—too much effort.

She began putting away her clothes, then, catching sight of her reflection, she walked close to the mirror and stood staring at herself. She looked different—alive. She had lost that sulky look she was aware she had developed. Her eyes were bright as well as her cheeks, and suddenly she remembered vividly that moment when she had looked into Larry's eyes on the dance floor.

She turned from the mirror, marched across the room, and went in search of Larry.

She found him in the sitting room, and as though expecting her, he had put two cups on the tray with the coffee pot. Farrell drank a cup of coffee and ate two of Mrs Adams' home-made biscuits and then she rose from her chair and murmured something about washing up the cups. She was disturbingly aware by now that she had not come from her room simply because she wanted a cup of coffee. She wanted more than that. She wanted—something unnamed from Larry. The realisation made her nervous. It was as though her desires had been spoken aloud even though she couldn't formulate them properly even to herself, and she turned aside from him as she stooped for the tray.

'Oh, leave it,' Larry said imperiously. 'Mrs Adams will see to all that in the morning.'

Farrell's heart began to beat fast. She straightened and faced him nervily, aware that he had risen and was moving towards her. He was lighting a cigarette, and as he shook out the match he looked at her steadily and disturbingly.

'You don't smoke, do you, Farrell?'

'No.' She added shakily, 'I—I thought *you* only smoked under stress.'

His eyes didn't move from her face. 'That's right. So I'm under stress now.'

'What—what do you mean?' Farrell stood perfectly still. Her pulses were racing and she had this crazy feeling she wanted to be back in his arms—here, in the seclusion of Quindalup, where she was no longer safe. To see how much she could take without freezing up—or fighting herself free. She asked, her voice low, vibrant, 'Why—why are you under stress?'

One corner of his mouth curled up slightly. 'Why do you think?'

She shook her head. 'I don't know.'

'Oh, come on now, Farrell. Of course you know.' He laughed briefly. 'Don't pretend you've forgotten what was happening between us on the dance floor tonight.'

'What?' she said huskily.

He frowned. 'You want me to say it? All right—to put it mildly, we wanted to go to bed with each other.'

Farrell's face went slowly scarlet. She was utterly shocked by his bluntness—by the knowledge that he thought she wanted that—that she was a girl who already knew all about going to bed with a man. For a mad moment, her instinct was to run. Then she swallowed hard and managed to say with icy coldness, 'As far as I'm concerned, you're—you're quite wrong. You must have been—imagining things.'

He smiled mockingly. 'Oh, Farrell! I'm not completely insensitive. I know when a girl's feeling amorous. There was urgency all over you—it was smouldering in your eyes—your fingers were wrestling with mine——'

'*My* fingers? You—it was *your* fingers that were—were——'

'Sending messages?' he suggested when she couldn't go on. 'Well, yours were certainly answering ... But you don't have to look so embarrassed about it all. I assure you, I'm very flattered. Still, I don't intend carrying you off to my bed tonight.' He drew on his cigarette, then asked her with sudden savagery, 'What kind of a lover was the man who left you? Was he passionate? Exciting? Did he——' He broke off abruptly and his tone changed. 'Suppose we both cool off outside, take a walk down by the water——'

Farrell scarcely heard him. She was so mortified she could have died, and she hated—*hated*—feeling this way. It was this warped idea she had been given by Aunt Jean that sexual feelings were shameful and debasing. She knew it was something she had to fight against, but all the same she couldn't—she simply couldn't—gather enough composure to go for a walk with Larry Sandfort just now—and tell him he was quite wrong about her 'lover', as she should. She shrank from his talk about passion, from the idea he had that she was eaten up with desire for him. Oh God— she couldn't ever feel that way about a man unless she was deeply in love with him, and even then—even then she didn't know if she would be able to let her emotions take over from her head. Bluntness, frankness, of the kind Larry was employing just didn't seem to help.

She moved a little, keeping her head bent, aware that her cheeks were still hectic.

'Thank you—but I don't need to cool down,' she said aloofly. 'And you can stop feeling flattered, Mr Sandfort. You're—you're quite mistaken about my—my feelings,' she floundered. She turned away from him swiftly. 'Goodnight,' she finished almost inaudibly.

Larry made no attempt to stop her from going, but it seemed to her that his 'Goodnight—and sleep well,' that followed her to the door had a note of mockery in it.

In her room, she pulled the curtains across the windows,

wondering as she did so if he would walk down to the water alone, smoking, perhaps, because he was—under stress, because he desired her. Her cheeks were still burning, and she turned quickly away when she caught a glimpse of her face in the mirror. She set to work to finish tidying her clothes away, wondering as she did so how long she—and Larry—would be staying here. Her emotions were so tangled she couldn't sort them out. She was deeply shocked that he thought she had been practically inviting him to go to bed with her.

Was *that* why he had decided to stay at Quindalup?

The sudden thought sent a tremor through her body. Hidden away here, what defence would she have if he chose to make love to her?

In the middle of folding a shirt, she dropped it and tip-toed nervously to the door. It had no lock, no bolt—she already knew that. She dragged a chair across, and then moved it away again. She was getting hysterical. Because somehow she knew that she could trust Larry. He had said, 'I don't intend to carry you off to my bed tonight', and she believed him. She need have no fears in that direction.

In bed at last, she lay sleepless, not bothered now as she had been last night by plans for escape. Bothered instead by a turmoil that had spread from her mind to her body, or perhaps the other way around—from her body to her mind. Those things Larry had said about her—her urgency, her amorousness—— And she had been so determined to impress on him that she had felt nothing, which wasn't true in the slightest degree. Held closely against him, aware of the stirrings in his own body, she had certainly made the discovery that she was not a cold frog. Yet he had supposed her stimulated in a way she had often been stimulated before. By Mark Smith.

If he only knew!

She shuddered a little and turned on her side, staring

into the black dark and listening to a silence that was intense. What did Larry intend to do? Of one thing she was becoming more and more certain. He would never again suggest that the way out of her dilemma was marriage with him. He had changed his mind about her merits. In fact, she was slowly reaching the conclusion that he could be in the process of handing over her place to Helen.

So why didn't he let her go?

CHAPTER EIGHT

IT was strange to get up in the morning knowing that he was there, that she would not have to spend the day alone with herself and her restless thoughts. She discovered he had asked Mrs Adams to serve breakfast in the garden, which made an unexpectedly agreeable start to the day. It provided an excuse for wearing sun-glasses too, and she found them useful to hide behind, because at the moment she felt a need to hide. She hadn't really recovered from their conversation of last night, though as far as Larry was concerned, it appeared to be completely forgotten, he was so calm and pleasant and matter-of-factly impersonal.

Mrs Adams was baking that morning, and Farrell decided to do some washing, partly out of necessity, partly from a desire to make herself unavailable for some perverse reason. Larry let her go her own way without questions, and from the laundry she saw him stride off in the direction of the electricity generator. He didn't appear again until, her washing hung out on the line, she was about to go inside the house.

He caught up with her on the verandah. 'How about a swim before lunch, Farrell?' he invited with a smile that was a combination of politeness and friendliness. The perfect host, she thought somewhat wryly. 'Or have you something further to do?'

'No. I'd like a swim,' she agreed. She couldn't, after all, avoid him for ever, and she didn't really want to.

'Fine. I'll be ready when you are.'

Farrell went to her room. She had been wearing her bikini here, while swimming on her own, but now she chose to put on a one-piece swimsuit patterned in pale apricot and brown. Her wardrobe consisted almost entirely of casual sun-clothes, because she had expected to be living at her father's resort hotel. If she'd landed a job in Port Hedland, or if she took one up anywhere in the near future, she would need to re-equip herself. As it was, the gear she had was ideal for Quindalup—terrace wear, sun-dresses, pants and an assortment of tops. For an instant she considered slipping on the robe that belonged to Helen, as a cover-up, but it didn't really go with her swimsuit, and as she had a long skirt that matched, she finally put that on. Then, slipping her feet into thongs and picking up her beach towel, she emerged from her room by the verandah door.

Larry was waiting for her, his muscular sun-tanned torso contrasting strongly with the white swim shorts he was wearing. She had a sudden vision of Mark, smaller, slimmer, similarly clad, standing by her bed, the towel around his neck concealing part of his scarred chest—— She shut off the image quickly, almost guiltily, and stared down the steps.

'You have some attractive clothes,' Larry commented as they walked through the shady garden. 'Is fashion one of your interests, Farrell?'

'Not really. I suppose I like clothes, but I never bothered much about fashion when I was in Perth.' She swished her long skirt pleasurably, feeling the fine cotton cool on her thighs and the backs of her legs. 'Most of my things are newish. I bought them specially to come to the North-West.'

'Your father footed the bill, I presume, since you were a student.'

She nodded. Was that a criticism, or was he—drawing her out? There wasn't much to discover about Farrell Fitzgerald. She'd hardly begun to live yet. She went on in case it was expected of her, 'Daddy made me an allowance all the time I was down south. My aunt managed it till a couple of years ago, and then I started to cope for myself. I never spent much on my back—I was too busy studying to have a social life, and Aunt Jean doesn't entertain. She likes books better than people.'

'And did you go along with that?' he quizzed.

'Till I realised there was an alternative,' she admitted seriously.

'Ah yes, of course,' he said dryly. They were walking by the water now, towards the sun shelter, and Farrell glanced at him through her lashes to see how she should take that. He returned her glance and commented, 'You certainly made big changes when you came to the North-West, didn't you?'

That was probably a reference to running away with a man, as he had once chosen to put it, but she decided to take it differently, though she flushed slightly.

'If you're referring to what Cecile said, I didn't intend to be lazy, you know. I planned to help my father at the hotel—and my stepmother too, of course. I'd only met her a couple of times, but I knew she had special interests of her own—she collects shells and all sorts of things to make really fascinating collages. I thought she might be pleased to have me around to take some of her tasks off her hands.'

She stood watching Larry as he strolled across the sea-grass matting that covered the floor of the sun shelter, and looked inside the small refrigerator. As well as the fruit juice and soft drinks that were usually there, Farrell noticed there were now bottles of various spirits as well as some cans of beer and a row of frosted glasses. He closed the door and picked up two li-los.

'Shall I put these outside, or do you prefer to come up here into the shade when you've had your swim? You have a nice tan, I see.'

'I generally dry off in the sun,' she said a little awkwardly.

As she followed him from the shelter, he remarked over

his shoulder, 'So you discovered your well-meant offers of help weren't so acceptable after all.'

'Yes. Well, Cecile seemed to think I was trying to up-stage her, or something.'

'And you weren't?' He set the li-los down and looked at her thoughtfully.

'Of course I wasn't! I thought Cecile and I would get along well together. I'd liked her—very much—when we met before. I just can't understand where it all went wrong.'

'No? Well, I can,' he said after a moment. 'I'll admit your stepmother's an attractive woman, Farrell, but she can't compete with youth.' He looked at her through narrowed eyes, and Farrell, who had unfastened the single button on her skirt, for some reason did it up again. 'You have a whole heap of attractions,' he resumed. 'If you give it some thought, it's natural that Cecile should want to be the undisputed leading lady in her husband's hotel.'

'Of course, I know that! I didn't want the limelight. I kept out of the way.' Farrell swung her towel and remembered how she had tried to do just that, how tactful she had been. Out of the blue, she recalled too that Cecile had accused her of butting in that day she had been having a drink with Larry Sandfort. She looked at him, opening her eyes wide. 'I suppose you think I was pushing my frame in that day I joined you and Cecile for a drink on the terrace. Did you think I was trying to win your attention away from her?'

'Now what on earth do you expect me say to that?' he said dryly. 'You know damned well I invited you to join us. In fact, you picked up my signal to you so quickly I took it as a sign.'

'A—a sign?' she repeated bewilderedly.

'Yes, a sign—that you were as much attracted to me as I was to you.'

Farrell stared at him. Had she been attracted to him? She knew she had. But she had definitely not been attracted in the way she suspected he meant.

'I felt it so strongly, I tell you I was stunned when I came back and found you gone,' he said after a pause.

She didn't know what to say, and told him uncomfortably, feeling she had been—and still was—naïve, 'I—I couldn't stay. You—you told me that yourself.'

'So I did.' His smile was ironic. 'But I told you, too, to wait for me . . . Well, are we going in the water?'

Farrell kicked off her thongs and discarded her skirt, and his eyes skimmed over her figure in a way that was vastly different from that time at her father's hotel. There was something hard in his eyes now, and though she had been wearing only a bikini then and was now far more covered up, she felt even more naked on this occasion than she had then. Rather quickly, she turned her back on him and walked down to the water. She felt he had made an unpleasant comment on her going away with another man, and had somehow underlined the implications by the way he had looked her over. How on earth could she explain to him that he was wrong about her relationship with Mark? She could hardly shout it out to him while they were swimming in the pool!

Neither could she come out with it over the cold drink he poured for her later, she discovered, because by that time, he was playing the considerate host again, talking of the beauties of Quindalup and suggesting that after lunch she might like to take a walk up the gorge with him.

'Have you discovered the lily pools yet, Farrell?'

'No.'

'Then you must see them. They're part of the unique charm of Quindalup. I expect you know many of the wildflowers. You'll have visited King's Park in Perth often enough, I'm sure.'

'Yes,' Farrell agreed, but had to admit that she didn't know many wildflowers by name. Such knowledge wasn't required for the exam subjects she had been expected to pass, she told him, and she had been too busy stuffing her head with essential facts to spare time for the inessential ones.

'Then a little of that won't go astray,' he said with a smile.

Farrell smiled back. It was almost impossible to believe that last night they had engaged in a very different kind of conversation...

That afternoon they walked into the gorge. It was completely different from the walks she had taken alone. In Larry's company, she was far more inclined to look around her and notice things she had been too distracted to bother with before. The steep rock walls were fiercely red, and contrasting with them were the pale gold of acacias and grevilleas, the whitened clumps of spinifex and the shining green of the wild fig trees. Crimson finches and crested pigeons fluttered in the snappy gums, and there were vivid splashes of colour on the ground where Sturt's Desert Pea flung the savage crimson of its flowers.

Pausing to admire the tender mauve of some mulla-mullas, Farrell discovered a spiky lizard, completely motionless except for the rapid movement of its tongue, as it dealt with a trail of busily running small black ants.

'That's a Mountain Devil,' Larry said from her side. They both watched for a while as the reptile, oblivious of their presence, licked its tongue rapidly in and out, whipping up one by one the tiny insects that formed its diet. Farrell found a deep fascination in watching nature this way, and remarked wonderingly as they moved on, 'You know, I never seem to have had time since I was a small child to stand and stare at things like that.'

'Pity,' he murmured, frowning slightly.

'Yes. I was too busy trying to keep pace with Aunt Jean's expectations,' she admitted ruefully. 'I was terrified I'd let the Roseblades down by not passing my exams. It's a wonder I don't need glasses! I always had my nose in a book except when I had them closed, committing to memory all the donkey bridges that were supposed to help me remember other strings of facts.'

He smiled sympathetically. 'Do you keep in touch with your aunt? Or have you cast her into outer darkness?'

'Oh no, I couldn't do that,' said Farrell, horrified. He held aside a trailing bunch of bougainvillea laden with flame-coloured flowers and she stooped and moved past him. 'I write to her. I had a letter from her the other day, as a matter of fact. She's made arrangements so I can go back to university next year if I want to.'

'And will you want to?'

'Never!' she said emphatically. 'I do love Aunt Jean, though. It might sound funny after some of the things I've said, but it's true. She never encouraged me to show it, though—demonstrativeness was frowned on. I was all inhibitions after a while. My parents were loving people, and it took me years to learn that hugs and kisses were out.'

'And now you're unlearning it?'

Farrell looked at him suspiciously, and blinked as he flicked a fallen flower from her hair.

'I'm *trying* to unlearn it,' she said, going on ahead again. 'It's not all that—easy.' Oh God, how did that sound? Would he take it as an invitation to help? She added quickly, 'But I'm managing all right.'

'I'm sure you are,' he agreed sardonically.

'Perhaps not as well as you imagine,' she said in a low voice. 'And not in the way you mean.'

Larry didn't answer, and she concluded, thankfully, that he hadn't heard her, because she felt she might soon be out of her depth.

'Just ahead,' he said, a few seconds later, 'beyond the Japanese bamboos, are the lily ponds.'

'They're well and truly hidden, aren't they?' she said, moving on eagerly. Half her eagerness was to escape conversation, even though the way it had been going it was leading in the direction she should have wanted it to take—where she could tell him outright that he was wrong about her and Mark.

She stood aside when he told her, 'Here, let me go in front—there's a way to get through this tangle——'

She followed him, and beyond the bamboos they came into what seemed a different world. High above, the red rocks towered, and Larry told her, 'Up there you might find some Tiger Eye if you cared to hunt for it. I'll show you the way up when we're on our way back.'

Presently they reached the lily ponds—a string of small and beautiful pools linked to each other by tiny cascades of lively crystal water. Pink lilies grew in two of them, and they were shaded and secret, as though belonging to some lost world. The water reflected the heavy thickets of bamboo, the bright tumble of bougainvillea, the white of the papery cadjeputs and the red of the enclosing rock walls.

'The bamboos aren't indigenous, as I suppose you realise,' Larry said, as Farrell stood entranced. 'They were planted here years ago, and because of the water they flourished. The same goes for the waterlilies.'

The waterlilies looked as if they belonged here. They floated serene and lovely on the shining water, and beneath them, the glassy green water-plants showed dazzlingly clear. It seemed to Farrell to be a long time since she had known a pleasure so intense as she felt now, and she glanced at Larry, wondering if he felt as she did, or if all this was too familiar to him. The strangely moody expression on his face made her realise that this was one of the places where he had planned they would discover each other. It was an utterly romantic place, and somehow he seemed to be very much a part of it.

Farrell, stooping to dip her fingers in the water, reflected that he was something of an enigma. Who would suspect so utterly masculine and realistic a man capable of making the kind of wildly romantic proposal he had once made to her? As well, there were the volumes of poetry on his bookshelves, and odd words and phrases he had used in speech to her floated back into her mind. 'I'll make your life a Song of Solomon'—'I'll love you and cherish you until the day I die' . . .

A shiver—a strange shiver of delight ran down her spine and glancing up, she caught his eye and stayed motionless for a timeless moment, her hand trailing in the glass-clear water. There was that expression in his eyes again—that expression that had drawn her to him the very first time she had ever seen him. Something madly romantic, madly idealistic . . . Was that what it was?

She straightened up slowly, her eyes not leaving his face, and then, abruptly, he moved and broke the spell. He picked up a small pebble and tossed it into the water, and reflection from the spreading ripples made flickers of light that danced across his face.

When he looked at her again there was a remoteness in his expression that chilled her.

'Shall we go?' he asked shortly, and without waiting for her to answer, he began to move away. Farrell followed him feeling strangely forlorn and rebuffed. He didn't want her here. Her idiotic musings had been right out of context, as far as he was concerned. Her mind turned to Helen, and she wondered if Larry was possibly thinking of her too, comparing the two girls to Farrell's disadvantage. Actually, she had no real idea whether Helen meant anything to him or not. Her inference that she did was based purely on that birthday card claiming her as his lovely Helen, and on Mrs

Adams' expectations that he would bring Helen back from Perth with him. It was very shaky evidence, when she looked at it sanely, in the light of day. She thought of saying casually, 'Now that you don't want me to marry you, is there someone else on your mind? Helen Adams, for instance?'

Instead, as they neared the thicket of bamboos, she asked him lamely, 'The Tiger Eye, Larry—will you show me the way up over the rocks?'

He paused and made a careless gesture. 'There where that patch of mullamullas is growing against the slope—do you see? The path starts there. It goes up to where the ghost gum's growing from that overhanging shelf of rock. That's the place to look.'

Farrell wanted to ask if they could climb up now, but she didn't, and though he asked, 'Do you want to make the climb now?' she sensed it was merely out of politeness, and that he didn't want to take her there. He had had enough of her.

'No, thank you,' she said carefully. 'I'll go on my own another time.'

'That wouldn't be wise,' he said sharply. 'You'll go with me, if you must go.'

But not today, she noted, as he resumed the trek back through the gorge with her following meekly behind.

He didn't offer to take her to look for Tiger Eye during the two days that followed either, nor did they go back to the lily ponds, though Farrell would have liked to do so. They swam, and they walked, and in the evenings they listened to music, talked generalities, and played a couple of games of Scrabble. On the whole, she found him surprisingly easy to be with, and there were often moments—long moments—when Farrell even felt she could live here, like this, for ever.

Mrs Adams never intruded. She might not have been

there, for the most part, except that the house was always cleaned, the meals were always prepared, there was always a supply of cold drinks both at the bungalow and in the sun shelter. Farrell began to understand to the full why Larry had been so sure they would get to know each other at Quindalup—as well as any couple who ever contemplated marriage. She understood even why he had claimed he could teach her to love him. Somehow here, in this beautiful lost world, such a thing could happen. Yet occasionally, generally at the very moment wheh they were most relaxed with each other, a constraint would come between them, and Farrell didn't know whether it was Mark or Helen who was at the root of it.

One evening after she had defeated him at Scrabble—she had learned he took defeat from a woman in very good part—he mixed a small jug of punch instead of settling for the usual coffee. Farrell watched interestedly as he combined dark rum with a mixture of lime, orange and pineapple juices, added a little sugar syrup, and shook it all up with crushed ice. The resultant drink, she presently discovered, was delicious, but when she had thirstily finished one tall glass of it and he offered her another, she shook her head laughingly.

'It has a definitely stupefying effect. If I have any more, I shan't be capable of taking myself off to bed.' As she smiled up at him, he reached out to take her hands and draw her to her feet, and she felt her heart begin to beat fast. He was going to kiss her, and she knew she badly wanted it to happen, and blamed her unexpected feeling of compliance on the punch.

But it didn't happen. She had lifted her head and half closed her eyes when suddenly, and quite inexplicably, Larry let her go. Her lids flew up and her cheeks burned. His eyes, that had been full of warmth a moment ago, were suddenly veiled, and somehow she was as certain as if he had told her that he was thinking of that other man—Mark Smith—making love to her. She felt an almost desperate compulsion to tell him the whole story, but before she could think how to begin, he let her hands slip out of his and told her with sudden aloofness, 'I guess you'd better take yourself off then, Farrell. Goodnight.'

There was nothing for her to do but to go, but in her room, long after she had gone to bed, she had a feeling of sick restlessness that kept her awake for a long time.

Next morning they walked into the gorge again, though they didn't go as far as the lily pools. It was a stifling hot day but pleasantly cool and restful in the shade of the trees that sheltered against the high red rock walls. Neither of them had anything much to say, Farrell because she was feeling languid with the heat and because she hadn't slept well the previous night, Larry because—well, how was she to know what kept him so quiet? She thought he had something on his mind, but she had no idea what it was. It could have been business, it could have been the problem of what to do with her, it could have been Helen Adams. At all events, he didn't want to talk, and proclaimed that he was looking for some particular wildflower that Mrs Adams wanted to incorporate in a painting she was doing. He didn't give Farrell a description of the flower, and after a while she wandered away from him, feeling slightly hurt. She had practically made up her mind to climb the path up the gorge wall to where he had said Tiger Eye was to be found when he called to her that he had found the flower he was looking for and they would go back to the bungalow.

They walked back almost in silence. Farrell hadn't enjoyed her morning and she felt like telling him so. She felt curiously aggrieved and unhappy, and she didn't really know why, unless it had something to do with the enervating heat. By the time they reached the house, she felt almost too exhausted to eat the salad that was laid out on a table in the cool of the verandah. She half expected Larry to say something about going back to Ansell over the meal, but he didn't.

She slept on her bed after lunch and woke when Larry knocked on the door and asked if she were coming for a swim.

It was still somnolently hot, and she splashed her face with cold water in the bathroom before getting into her black bikini. On an impulse, she put the yellow and white robe around her shoulders before she went to join him at the pool. The birthday card was no longer in the pocket—she had put it in the top drawer of the dressing table, as she had worn the robe several times before Larry came. She passed Mrs Adams painting on the verandah and stepped out in the heat that seemed to have increased, so that the earth glowed dull red and there was a heaviness like reflections from copper in the hazy sky.

When she found Larry, he was carrying two li-los from the shelter, to set up on the very edge of the water in the shade of the trees. He wore brief oatmeal-coloured swimming shorts that looked pale against his darkly tanned body and legs. Conscious of the robe she was wearing, Farrell stood and watched him, waiting till he had turned and seen her before she began to slip it off. Slight colour rose in her cheeks as his glance took in the garment, but his expression didn't change and he made no comment.

She tossed the robe down so carelessly it fell on the ground, and she was aware of intense frustration. Why didn't he say something? Yet what had she expected? That he'd be angry to see her in Helen's robe? That he'd look startled, or even guilty? But why should he?

He had told her that night at the Lobster Pot that she'd be able to ask him any questions she liked at Quindalup— that he'd answer her honestly. But she could hardly hold him to such a promise now, because they were at Quindalup under very different circumstances from the ones he had been envisaging then. With a feeling of futility, she left the robe where it had fallen and went into the water.

She was floating on her back, her eyes closed, when she became aware that Larry was near her. Opening her eyes, she saw him, chest-deep in the water, his hair darkened, his eyelashes wet.

'Is it going to storm?' she asked him languidly.

'Not a chance. It's just one of those oppressive days that knock you to pieces. This is the best place to be. You'll feel better when your blood's cooled down.'

'I expect so,' she agreed on a breath.

They stayed in the water for some time, swimming, floating, drifting, scarcely speaking. On the surface, it was not so different from other days, yet Farrell knew that it was not the same at all. The silence between them was loaded, it was no longer comfortable. Larry left the water before she did, but after a few minutes she followed him, though she hadn't meant to. He was stretched out on his back on one of the li-los, his eyes closed, and for a moment she stood looking at him. A moment that seemed like an eternity.

She had seen him half-naked like this often enough, so nothing was different. Yet suddenly everything was different. For some inexplicable reason, today, the sight of his narrow hips, his broad muscular chest, the hairs on his thighs shining golden in the sun, set her pulses racing. A dazed and paralysing weakness crept into every part of her body, so that it required an immense effort for her to take the few steps that brought her to the other li-lo, and commit herself to it. As she lay there, she had a vivid and almost tangible sensation of being held against Larry's body. Her breath caught in her throat and she closed her eyes and bit hard on her lip. Last night, she had wanted him to kiss her, but now——

Oh God! Had she fallen in love with him?

There were leaping flames along her nerves, and when she opened her eyes, Larry was sitting up, looking at her. Something told her that he knew—heaven knew how— what she was feeling. Just as he had known that night in Ansell when they were dancing. But he didn't—couldn't— know why she was feeling it. Or that in just a few days Quindalup had worked some spell on her so that she had become—addicted to his company, and worse. Something that he *didn't* now want to happen . . .

Her breast rose and fell and there was perspiration on her forehead, on her upper lip, and under her eyes. Because it was hot? But hadn't her blood been cooled by the water?

Larry, sitting on the edge of the li-lo, his hands on his knees, continued to stare at her. Farrell had the most peculiar sensation of being naked. Her hands tingled as if they must move—to cover a nakedness that didn't exist. It was only with a tremendous effort that she forced herself to lie still with Larry looking at her the way he was.

'Tell me something, Farrell,' he said almost musingly, narrowing his eyes now and thereby releasing her from the spell that seemed to be holding her. 'Exactly what were you after when you left Perth? You've told me sufficient about the set-up there for me to catch on you didn't have a lot of fun. Were you out to make up for lost time—to lash out and experiment with all the things that had been, I take it, forbidden to you then?'

Farrell shook her head, making an effort at composure. She forgot her feeling of nakedness as she groped for words to answer him, confused as she was by his questions, his insinuations. 'I—I just wanted to—to find myself, to make my own decisions. To—to choose for myself what I wanted to do, not to be—led. I admire my aunt—her coolness, her remoteness, her—dedication. But I don't want to be—I *can't* be—like that. So——'

'I see,' he said, when she paused. He was looking at her

differently now, narrowly, thoughtfully. 'Then if it wasn't simply a matter of throwing yourself headlong into sexual experiments—you thought yourself in love with this man you ran away with? Is that it?'

Farrell had a feeling of helplessness. She sat up, swinging her feet to the ground, knowing she had coloured. It looked as if her opportunity to tell him the truth about herself and Mark was right here, at this instant, and it seemed important she shouldn't miss it. She said with slow deliberation, looking him straight in the face, 'I didn't run away with him. You keep saying that, but I didn't. I just—I had to get myself out of Cecile's hair, and this chance came up to get to Port Hedland, so I—I took it. That's all.'

Larry listened without comment, but his look was sceptical, and Farrell realised that to him, it wasn't nearly as simple as she had tried to make out. After all, she had deceived her father—and she had shared a room with Mark. That latter point was the cause of the whole problem, so perhaps if she made light of it——

She drew a deep breath and continued, 'We both just happened to be looking for work—he didn't mind giving me a lift.'

He raised his eyebrows. 'Then why didn't you stay in Port Hedland if you were seriously looking for work, instead of—— Good God, Farrell,' he exclaimed explosively, 'you came inland, where you must surely have known you'd have the devil's own job finding any kind of work at all. You were sharing a room with this man who—merely gave you a lift.'

She was pale now, and she twisted her hands together nervously. 'Yes, but—but that doesn't mean we——' She stopped and tried again, wishing she had the sophistication not to falter. 'We didn't—he didn't——'

'He didn't *what*? Make love to you? Is that what you mean?'

She nodded desperately. 'There was nothing—nothing like that.' To her shame, she flushed painfully as she said it, aware that it was not altogether true, particularly from Mark's angle. Aware too that his eyes were taking in every fleeting expression that crossed her face.

'You mean,' he said, after a moment, 'that there was not even a kiss, not a skirmish—in bed or out of it—between you? I find that more than a little hard to swallow.' His glance travelled with slow thoroughness over her body, and down the slender length of her suntanned legs, then returned to her face, her cap of curling fair hair already dried by the heat of the sun and wisping delicately over her forehead. He smiled crookedly. 'A man wouldn't even need to be in love with you to want to possess your body, Farrell— and you certainly put temptation in his way. Your boyfriend would have to be either decidedly undersexed or to have more self-control than is usual to leave you untouched, and from your stepmother's comments, I gathered he was perfectly normal.' His eyes found hers and searched them deeply. 'Why have you waited till now to protest your innocence? Why didn't you speak up that day I found you in Ansell, if I maligned you?'

'You didn't give me a chance, you—you jumped to conclusions,' she said. And she, she remembered, still unnerved by that king-sized pass Mark had made at her the night before, and by his disappearance in the morning—she had looked so guilty there was only one possible conclusion for him to have jumped to. 'You're a—a cynic,' she said wearily.

'You're quite right, I am a cynic. Unfortunately, when I'm not being a cynic I'm a romantic. And there, if you're interested, is my dilemma. The romantic in me finds the ideal, the cynic points out the feet of clay.'

Farrell looked at him wordlessly. Had he seen her as an ideal—when she was merely a hopelessly inexperienced girl apt to make the stupidest of mistakes? She shook her head bewilderedly.

'What was the idea in sharing a bedroom, for God's sake? What would anyone think? And don't tell me it was a matter of economy. Your father wouldn't let you go short of cash.'

Farrell's heart sank. Her determination to set the record straight didn't seem to be going too well at all. 'There was only one vacancy at the hotel in Port Hedland,' she said on a sigh, knowing now, when it was far too late, how foolish she had been. 'There was nothing else to do.'

He grimaced. '*He* told you that, I suppose, and you believed it.'

'Yes—because it was true,' she said obstinately. Had it been true, though? She really had no idea, and she wondered what her eyes were telling him. *His* eyes were sending her a message that was very plain to read. He didn't believe a word she said . . .

Suddenly she exclaimed frustratedly, 'Oh, what's the use? You can believe what you like. I don't care. If you choose to think I'm a liar, or anything else, I can't help it. I know I'm not perfect, but then neither is anyone, and I'm sick of having you grill me. I—I could ask *you* a whole lot of embarrassing questions too, if I thought I had any right.'

'Go ahead, then,' he said, frowning. 'You have as much right as I have to ask questions.'

'Exactly. That's just what I mean. You don't have any right.'

'Oh, quit making an argument of it! We're not playing some game where all the rules are laid out and have to be adhered to . . . What did you want to ask me? Come on, let's have it. What's the question?'

Farrell bit her lip. What *was* the question? She swallowed nervously. She wanted to know about Helen Adams, of course—if she was a possible contender for the role of his wife, particularly now that Farrell Fitzgerald had been found to have feet of clay.

She reached down and picked up the silky robe from where it lay in a crumpled heap on the ground, then let it fall again. 'This was in the wardrobe in my room,' she began, and stopped, her cheeks bright with sudden colour.

'So what? It belongs to my housekeeper's daughter-in-law, Helen.'

He sounded so convincingly casual that Farrell was almost fooled, and might have been completely so if she hadn't found that rather—possessive card in the pocket.

'Where is she now?' she challenged.

'In Perth. She works for my company.'

'She's—she's a widow, isn't she?'

'Yes,' he said shortly, unhelpfully.

'You—like her a lot, don't you?' she persisted after a second.

'Now how on earth did you deduce that?' he asked, his eyes guarded.

Farrell bit her lip. So he didn't deny it! 'Various things I picked up,' she said evasively, deciding he could take that to mean whatever he liked. 'She's very lovely, I suppose,' she added, thinking of the birthday card.

'Very lovely,' he agreed. 'But not nearly so lovely as you. And not so damned devious, either.'

Farrell felt a pulse beat in her temple. 'Then perhaps you'd be——' She stopped on the point of suggesting he'd be better off with Helen than with her, because after all, he was making no claim to *her*, these days, even if he was keeping her captive at Quindalup.

'I'd be what?' he said. 'Finish what you were going to say.'

She improvised swiftly. 'More inclined to trust her than

you are to trust me. Or—or was she another ideal your cynicism knocked down from her pedestal?'

'As a matter of fact, no,' he said evenly. He got up from the li-lo and stood looking down at her, his hands on his naked hips. He was too close for comfort, and she averted her eyes quickly. 'Why the interest, anyhow?'

Why? Farrell hadn't really questioned her interest herself up till now, but in a flash, she knew the answer. Because she was eaten up with jealousy! She'd thought she hated Larry Sandfort not so long ago, and now, quite unfairly, she found she was hating Helen Adams.

'Well?' said Larry, and she tried to pull herself together.

'Because—oh, because I believe she's coming to the North-West for a holiday,' she said weakly. 'Mrs Adams said something about it.'

'I don't quite follow your reasoning, but yes, she'll be coming to Mullamulla Downs shortly. She doesn't have a close relationship with her mother-in-law. She'll spend most of her time with her parents.'

Farrell frowned. 'Her—parents?' she repeated.

'Sure. Bob and Muriel Nelson. Muriel in particular appreciates her company these days, since Mark walked out on them.'

Farrell stared at him, feeling confused. So Helen was Larry's manager's daughter, and Mark——

'Mark?' she echoed faintly, feeling an odd stirring of unease.

'Their son,' Larry explained patiently. 'One of these wild kids who can't settle down. He was working for his father, but decided he didn't like being told what to do. Now he doesn't even find it necessary to keep in touch.'

Farrell's heart seemed to skip a beat. It sounded exactly like Mark Smith. *His* father owned a sheep station, and Mark couldn't settle down either. Nor did he keep in touch with his parents, she remembered. But this was Mark

Nelson, she reminded herself sharply, not Mark Smith. Yet was Mark's name really Smith, or did he call himself that so as not to be traced? She felt slightly dizzy, and she moved nervously, aware that Larry was watching her intently. She had completely lost track of what she had been asking him, and she started when he asked out of the blue, 'Why did your boy-friend leave you, Farrell? That's something I can't understand.'

Farrell pulled her thoughts back from their mad peregrinations. She had a horribly clear picture of what had happened that night at the roadhouse—Mark's kisses, his fingers fumbling with her pyjama jacket. She could hear her own scream that had been stifled instantly, and her heart was thudding now as it had then.

'We—we disagreed,' she said, her voice low.

'About what?'

She should have said, 'He wanted to make love to me and I didn't want him to,' but she couldn't say it. She felt too ashamed. Instead, she answered with a shrug, 'Oh—I wanted to go back to Port Hedland and he wanted to go on to Meekatharra. Something like that.'

It was an evasion and it sounded like one. Larry muttered something under his breath, then stooped to pick up Helen Adams' robe. He tossed it over her scarcely covered body and went back to the house.

Farrell stared after him helplessly. It seemed a pretty fair indication of his contempt for her and her—deviousness. So she had better rid herself of this idea that she was becoming at all attached to him.

If she could . . .

CHAPTER NINE

IN the morning when she came out to breakfast, Mrs Adams greeted her with the news that Larry had gone out for the day. She didn't volunteer any information as to where he had gone, and Farrell couldn't help wondering if it was to meet Helen. Reason told her it was unlikely, for he had said merely that Helen would be coming shortly, and she didn't see how he could have suddenly discovered it was today, but all the same, she felt nervous and unsettled.

'What about me?' she wondered forlornly when, her breakfast completed without appetite, her room tidied, she wandered down to the sun shelter and flung herself full length on one of the li-los, to stare broodingly out at the glittering water and the tree shadows that fell sombrely across the red of the earth. It was not so oppressively hot as yesterday, but she hadn't the energy to swim, and besides, her mind was possessed by thoughts of Larry and her own dilemma. He was finished with her, that much was becoming very plain. As for herself, she wondered now whether, ever since he had come to her rescue in the saloon bar at Ansell, she hadn't in her heart been longing for him to repeat his proposal of a few weeks ago. From the very start—she admitted it now—she found him intriguing, and who knows—if Cecile hadn't made those rather terrifying remarks about his passionate nature, she just might have hung on at home until he had come back.

Oh God, there were so many things to regret now. She suspected that she was here only because Larry had, for some reason, made himself responsible for her, and written to her father to that effect. If only—if only she could con-

154

vince him that at least as far as her behaviour with Mark
was concerned, she didn't have feet of clay! If she could
have just one more chance ...

All morning she gave no more than a passing thought to
Mark Smith who was very possibly Mark Nelson. It didn't
seem to have a great deal of relevance one way or the other,
and it wasn't until the afternoon, when for want of some
better way to pass the time she took a walk into the gorge,
that her thoughts returned to the subject.

It would be a very odd coincidence if he were Mark
Nelson, she thought, as she sat down on a large red rock in
the shade of the cadjeputs. Momentarily diverted, she
watched a trail of ants hastening purposefully across a
patch of bare earth, and reflected that they could unknow-
ingly be heading for disaster in the form of a waiting
mountain devil. People were like that too, she mused, the
way they rushed heedless into danger. When she had hurried away from her father's home, for instance, she had
built up more trouble for herself than she would ever have
imagined. She had seen nothing dangerous about Mark, she
had been as foolish and trusting as some naïve schoolgirl
until the night he had tried to claim what he had thought
she offered when she went away with him.

Oh yes, she thought, gazing thoughtfully into space.
Larry's 'wild kid' and Mark Smith could quite easily be
one and the same person. Farrell frowned a little as she
tried to call up all she knew about Mark. He'd said he had
a sister who lived in Perth and came home for holidays, and
she was almost certain he had said her name was Helen. He
hadn't said she was a widow, though, or mentioned that her
husband had been killed in a plane accident.

With that thought, something else fell into place. Those
scars on Mark's body. Larry had said his manager's son had
gone up with Brian Adams—that he had been hurt. It must
be the same person! No wonder he hadn't wanted to talk

about how he had got those scars. It must have been a terrible experience, especially as it was his brother-in-law who was killed. Poor Helen!

Yes, but poor Helen had evidently recovered sufficiently to be comforted by Larry Sandfort's admiration for her. The fact she kept his card surely meant something, and anyhow, what girl wouldn't be flattered by the attentions of such a man? Farrell had been flattered herself—she had been stunned, in fact. Stunned and disbelieving. Well, in her case, the admiration hadn't lasted long. *She* had blotted her copybook—so he thought. Helen had not.

How confused and muddled her life was becoming! But no doubt it would all end very simply. Farrell had only to tell Larry she had decided to go back to her aunt in Perth and he would let her leave without a regret. And that, she supposed with a sigh, was what she would do. It was no use prolonging the agony.

It was mainly to divert herself from her depressing thoughts that presently, as she wandered past the mulla-mullas, she took it into her head to climb the steep path up the gorge wall. It would be fun to find some Tiger Eye. She had seen rings and pendants made of the beautiful stone that glittered golden like the eye of a tiger, and if she found some it would be a souvenir—something to remind her of the days she had spent at Quindalup.

The path, she soon discovered, was treacherous. After the first slope, it was against the sheer rock face, and she tried not to look down, and grasped gratefully at a branch of one of the small wiry trees that grew there, whenever she could. Now and again, small bits of rock gave way under her feet, and soon she began to wish she hadn't been so reckless as to start the climb. She wasn't at all sure if she was following the right path, and she tried not to think of what it would be like to go down. She paused to rest after negotiating a very narrow nerve-racking stretch, and looked up to see how far she had yet to go to reach the snappy gum that Larry had pointed out to her. The movement made her suddenly dizzy, she swayed slightly, staggered and the next instant a great chunk of rock went hurtling down into the gorge. Exactly how it happened she never knew, but she lost her footing completely and with a sense of intense shock she felt herself falling, falling——

She grasped futilely at the rock face, her mind emptied of all thought by sheer fright. A bit of stone hurtled past her, another followed, something struck her on the head and just before she blacked out she felt her body slump into something springy and prickly. It was a native bush, and it probably saved her life, but she didn't know that until much later.

It seemed she was wandering lost in a sort of half dark for a long, long time, and she didn't know what was real and what was dream—or nightmare. She was looking for Larry. She wanted to beg him to believe her, not to leave her alone. She thought she saw him looking at her from the other side of a sheet of water, but the light on it dazzled her eyes so much that she couldn't see. She called his name. 'Larry?'

'What's the trouble?' His voice had a strange unreal echo to it as if it came from a long way off.

'Please—please help me!'

'When you've lied to me?'

She began to weep. 'It's true—it's true. I wouldn't let him touch me——'

'Mark? Mark Nelson?' Larry asked mockingly, and then the man across the water was Mark after all. Farrell knew it, because she could see the scars on his chest, and she gasped out, 'You *are* Mark Nelson, aren't you?'

Suddenly he was right beside her and had put his hand over her mouth. 'Don't tell them,' he said threateningly. He seized one of her wrists with fingers that were icy cold, and she struggled against him, trying in vain to push him away.

'Keep still, Farrell.'

It wasn't Mark's voice now, and Farrell opened her eyes. The man who was bending over her and holding her wrist was a stranger, and she was in her room at Quindalup.

'Who—are you?' she asked weakly, and then she saw Larry.

'It's all right, Farrell. This is Dr Carter from Quindalup——'

'Take it easy,' the doctor soothed. 'You've been fighting me off a bit—must have been dreaming. I've just been making sure you're all in one piece. You've got a few scratches we'll have to clean up, but no bones broken ... Any headache?'

'A—a little,' Farrell said huskily, aware now that her head was throbbing. It was all coming back to her—the fall in the gorge, that blow on her head—— She put her hand to her temple and discovered a lump that hurt. 'How did I get here? What time is it?' she asked confusedly.

'It's nine o'clock at night, and Larry here found you, pet. Now how about having a sip or two of this nice warm drink Mrs Adams has made for you and swallowing this tablet for me?'

Farrell did as she was told. Larry was looking at her so kindly and concernedly that she wanted to cry, so she closed her eyes. Though her head ached, she didn't feel muddled, only weak and rather vague. She heard the murmur of voices—'No need for hospital—very lucky—a few scratches and bruises—quiet—sleep—a slight concussion—Lesley keep an eye on her—a few days——' The words were blurring, becoming senseless as she lapsed into a more comfortable unconsciousness again ...

That night and the following day passed with a kind of timelessness. She knew Mrs Adams was looking after her, and she saw Larry smiling at her once or twice, but it was all very unreal. It was a relief to wake the next morning to full consciousness, without the dizzying feeling that she had dragged herself only half way out of some other ephemeral world. Her head no longer ached, and she felt faint but definite pangs of hunger.

Doctor Carter arrived to see her soon after she had finished her breakfast, and pronounced himself very satisfied with her progress. After warning her she would have to take it easy for several days yet, he took his leave, and Mrs Adams, having seen him off, came back into the room.

'I'd like to get up, please,' said Farrell. She hadn't seen Larry so far and she wondered where he was, and thought she might have a better chance of finding out—and of thanking him for coming to her rescue—if she were up and about. But she soon found she needed Mrs Adams' help in bathing and dressing, for her bruised body was stiff and sore. She looked ruefully in the mirror when she was dressed, and discovered herself pale and shadowy-eyed, the dressings on her temple and one hand, that had been cut by sharp rocks during her fall, giving her a slightly battered appearance. She certainly didn't look very attractive, and what a nuisance she was making of herself! At this rate, Larry would be more than glad to see her go—yet she couldn't forget the way he had seemed to look at her so kindly while she was lying in bed.

In any case, whether it made sense or not, she was aching to see him again as she tottered out to the verandah. There, Mrs Adams had arranged a long cushioned lounger for her, and beside it, on a low table, were a few magazines, a glass, and a jug of fruit juice.

'Where's Larry?' Farrell asked, as she thankfully sank down on the lounger, very much aware that she was far from capable of being normally active as yet, and acknowledging that she would have to stay at Quindalup a few days more at the least.

'Mr Sandfort's gone to take a swim. He'll come and spend some time with you when he comes back to the house, Miss Fitzgerald. He didn't want to disturb you earlier. Doctor Carter said you must rest up and be quiet for a while yet, you know.'

Farrell made a slight grimace. 'I feel a fraud. After all, I haven't broken any bones—not a single one. And I'm giving you such a lot of extra work, Mrs Adams. I've messed up your arrangements completely, haven't I? ... Oh, and wasn't it Sunday yesterday?' she added, remembering. 'Your husband was home and you had to spend all your time on me.'

Mrs Adams smiled pleasantly. 'Don't worry, Miss Fitzgerald. As a matter of fact, Jim didn't come home this weekend, and even if he had, you've been so undemanding it would have been no bother at all.'

When she had gone, Farrell stayed where she was, though she longed to go into the garden and wander in the direction of the sun shelter, just so that she could see Larry. It was almost unbearable to know he was so close and yet she couldn't even see him. Resignedly, she reached for a magazine ...

She didn't know how it happened, but the lounger was so comfortable that she must have fallen asleep. She opened her eyes at a slight sound to find Larry leaning against the verandah rail and watching her, an unreadable expression on his face.

He moved and came towards her, smiling.

'How's the patient today?'

'Oh, I'm not a patient,' she protested. Her heart was beating fast as she met his eyes, and she realised to the full what a deep and extraordinary pleasure it gave her simply to look at him. His hair was wet, and he looked healthy and handsome in an open-weave cream tussore short and light-coloured cotton trousers. 'I'm—I'm just about better now.

I'm sorry for all the bother I've been, and I haven't even thanked you yet for rescuing me,' she raced on. 'I know I shouldn't have climbed up there—you warned me not to. I—I don't quite know why I did it, except I wanted to have a piece of Tiger Eye to keep as a souvenir when——' She broke off, biting her lip. 'Where did you go? To—to Ansell?'

He shrugged his broad shoulders and lowered himself into a chair. 'I didn't go anywhere in particular. Just away from you.'

'Away from me?' she echoed, startled.

'Yes. I had some thinking to do and the best idea seemed to be to get away from all distractions.'

Farrell frowned slightly. 'You have—business worries?' she asked tentatively.

'Business worries?' Larry smiled crookedly. 'No, I had to think about you, Farrell. Didn't you guess that?'

'About *me*?' She stared at him and felt swift colour rush to her cheeks. But of course—she had to think what was to be done with her, that was all he meant. She said with a sigh, 'You don't have to feel responsible for me. I'll write and tell my father——'

He looked at her quizzically. 'Is that what you've decided? You'll go quite happily?'

Oh God, no—she wouldn't go happily at all! She wished and wished that he would insist he couldn't let her go—that she must stay—that they would start all over at the beginning again. But he insisted on no such thing, and, eyes lowered, she told him, 'It's the best thing to do.'

'Well, we'll see,' he said after a moment. 'But one thing's for sure—you're not leaving this place until you're one hundred per cent fit again. Doctor's orders are that you keep quiet and don't upset yourself—you've had a slight concussion, you know. So we'll forget all about future moves for the time being, and when you're really better, you and I are going to have a long talk.' He smiled and got to his feet, then stood looking down at her, an odd expression on his face. 'Just one thing—I accept what you told me the other day. About yourself and—Mark. That's his name, isn't it? You were having quite a conversation with him when the doctor came the other night.'

'Was I?' Farrell's head was spinning. She wondered, in slight alarm, what she had said, but she didn't really feel greatly concerned, because *Larry believed her*! That seemed terribly important, and her heart was racing. 'What did I say?' she asked lightly.

'Oh, nothing terribly coherent,' Larry told her, and with an enigmatic smile he went into the house.

Not much later, Mrs Adams came out and laid a table for lunch on the verandah, and when lunch was over, the housekeeper insisted she must go to her room and rest. It was the last thing Farrell wanted to do—she wanted to spend the afternoon with Larry—but the fact was, she needed to rest, as she discovered when she got to her feet and was overtaken by an attack of dizziness. Reluctantly, she went to her room, and once she was lying down, she barely had time to remind herself that Larry believed in her innocence before she fell asleep.

When she woke, it was after four. She bathed her face and got into her long flowered skirt and a long-sleeved shirt, and brushed her hair. She felt slightly shaky and she was conscious of the bruises on her body and limbs, and of a throbbing ache under the dressing at her temple. As she came on to the verandah from her room, she heard a car door slam, a motor rev up, and then she saw a taxi moving down the gravel road in the direction of Ansell. Voices became audible as she stood unmoving outside her bedroom door.

'Oh, Larry, how I adore this big old place!' a woman's voice exclaimed. 'I just want to give it one great big hug and a kiss ... I rang home, you know, from the airfield, and they said you were here, so I came straight out. There are lots of things I'm longing to talk to you about before I see anyone else at all.'

Footsteps sounded on the verandah, and Farrell retreated hastily to her room. Her heart was pounding, her throat dry. She knew the visitor must be Helen Adams, and she felt sick with jealousy. She wanted to go back to bed again, to lapse into sleep—not to wake up until Helen had gone. Except that when Helen went, Larry obviously would go too—and not only because Helen didn't have her own transport. There was no doubting the proprietorial note in that rather wooing, very feminine voice.

She was sitting on the edge of the bed shivering and hating herself she didn't know how many minutes later when Mrs Adams knocked and came in.

'Oh, you're up, Miss Fitzgerald. Afternoon tea's ready in the garden—and we have another visitor.'

Farrell looked at her, her grey-green eyes darkening. 'Who is it?' she asked, though she already knew.

'Helen Adams.' Oddly, the housekeeper didn't say, 'My daughter-in-law'.

'Oh—well, I—I don't think I'll interrupt. I'll have a cup of tea here, if it's not too much trouble.'

Mrs Adams shook her head. 'I'm sorry, dear, but Mr Sandfort wants you to join them.'

Farrell hesitated on the point of protesting that she didn't feel up to it, but what was the use? She would have to meet Helen—lovely Helen—some time and, despite everything she was curious to meet her, even though it would be rubbing salt in the wound. Bracing herself, she went across the verandah and into the garden. There, in the shade of a poinciana tree, Helen was pouring tea, turned slightly away from Farrell. A dark-haired girl, tallish, slender——

Larry, aware of Farrell's approach, stood up and smiled, and Helen put down the teapot and turned her head and stared. Farrell saw with a feeling of positive shock a strong resemblance to Mark—the dark eyes, the bone structure, the straight nose. Mark was good-looking and Helen was —yes, she was lovely, in a cool, chiselled, flawless way.

'Come along and sit down, Farrell,' said Larry. In a couple of strides he was beside her and had taken her arm. Farrell pulled away without meaning to. She knew she had gone pale and she was trembling a little. 'Are you all right?' Larry asked.

'Of course I am!' she said with forced brightness. She gazed back at Helen, whose dark eyes, so like Mark's it was uncanny, were fixed curiously on her, and went from the dressing on her brow to her bandaged hand.

'This is Farrell Fitzgerald, Helen,' Larry said. 'Farrell— Helen Adams. Helen's just flown up from Perth and is on her way to holiday with her parents at Mullamulla Downs.'

'Oh, of course—you're Mrs Adams' daughter-in-law,' Farrell said nervously, managing a smile, but the other girl frowned, obviously not pleased by this method of placing her.

'I was Helen Nelson—my father manages Larry's sheep station for him,' she said coolly. 'Sit down, won't you? Do you take milk in your tea?'

'Yes, please.' Farrell sat down and there was a little pause while Helen poured another cup and Larry handed it to Farrell, then offered her the sugar.

'Farrell Fitzgerald,' Helen said slowly and thoughtfully, then, as Larry sat down, she turned her lovely dark eyes on him and make a little grimace. 'Have I caught you out in an—indiscretion, Larry?'

'Not at all,' he said sharply. 'Farrell's been having a much-needed spell here. And if you're wondering—she had a fall in the gorge the other day, which accounts for her various bruises and scratches and her somewhat bandaged appearance.'

'Oh dear, what bad luck! But you shouldn't have left your invalid's couch on my account,' Helen said sweetly. 'Larry and I were just about to embark on a heart-to-heart talk,' she added pointedly.

In other words, 'You are intruding', thought Farrell. But Mrs Adams had said Larry wanted Farrell to join them. That, she reminded herself, was probably to bring her out in the open, so that Helen wouldn't think he had anything to hide. And of course he had not. She glanced at Larry rather anxiously, and he said off-handedly, 'Don't feel yourself *too* hamstrung, Helen. You'll stay tonight, won't you?'

'May I?' Helen raised her eyebrows as she said it. 'I don't want to intrude,' she added not very pleasantly.

'You're not doing that.' Larry sounded annoyed. 'If it's not too much of a secret, what's the news you were about to break, anyhow? I'm sure Farrell will excuse us for returning to the point where she joined us ... Have a lamington, Farrell,' he added, passing the plate of home-made cakes.

Farrell took one out of nervousness, for she didn't feel at all hungry, and the sight of the square of sponge cake liberally coated with chocolate icing and coconut made her feel slightly sick.

Helen drank some of her tea before she took up Larry's question, and Farrell suspected she was put out by her presence. She wondered rather crazily what Helen would say if she told her, 'By the way, Helen, I know your brother Mark. As a matter of fact, we——'

Her thoughts broke off abruptly as the other girl said, 'It was about Mark, Larry. I'm aware you've been trying to keep track of him for Mother's sake ever since he left home, but do you happen to know where he is just now?'

'As a matter of fact, no,' said Larry. 'The last time I managed to trace him he was working on a prawning trawler up on the north coast. That was several weeks ago, and since then I've had other things on my mind.' The blueness of his gaze glinted swiftly in Farrell's direction, then returned to Helen. 'However, I have an idea that he's now working his way south.'

Farrell was sitting quite still. So that 'private investigation' that had brought Larry to the Coral Reef Hotel had been to check up on Mark! But what had given him the idea Mark was now working his way south? She didn't look at him, and now Helen was speaking again.

'You're quite right, Larry. He hasn't been all alone, though—he's had a girl with him. And you'll never guess what——'

She paused, but Larry said nothing. Farrell went red and then white, and lowered her head to hide her agitation, pretending to be intent on brushing crumbs from her skirt. Oh God, what on earth was Helen going to say next? How much did she know? Yet reason said she couldn't possibly know that the girl with Mark had been Farrell Fitzgerald, or surely she'd have said so before this. All the same, there had been something decidedly strange in the slow way she had repeated Farrell's name a little while ago. Farrell waited in an agony for her to go on.

'Well, let's hear it,' said Larry, setting his cup on the table and looking hard at Helen.

'He wants to get a job and settle down! He's reached the conclusion that the free and easy life is not so free and easy after all.'

Farrell let out a slow breath of relief—somewhat prematurely, as she all too soon was to discover.

'I'm glad to hear it,' said Larry. 'What does he plan to do? Frankly, I very much doubt he'd ever make the grade jackerooing at Mullamulla Downs. Muriel would love it, but I don't think he and Bob will ever be able to work together—there've been too many serious clashes between them.'

'Don't worry, he doesn't want that, Larry. Actually, he's hoping you'll wangle something for him with Ansell-Sandfort Mining. You know—something with a nice house and good pay, but *not* sweating in the dust out at the mountain.'

Larry's mouth twisted sardonically. 'You've seen him, have you?'

'Yes. He turned up in Perth a couple of days ago and came to see me at the office. I was rather busy, but he got the essentials across, and I promised I'd ask you.'

Larry's eyes had narrowed. 'Just how serious is he? Because it's not my policy to employ—hangers-on.'

'He's *really* serious. Honestly. As a matter of fact—hang on to your hat, Larry, because here comes the punch line —he wants to get married!'

'What? *To whom?*' Larry shot out.

'To this girl he's been with, of course.'

Farrell stifled a gasp, and her senses reeled. She leaned back in her chair, feeling completely stunned. It just couldn't be true! Mark had never shown the slightest sign of wanting to marry her. Could he have been making it all up simply to persuade Larry to give him a job? Was Mark like that? She glanced across at Larry. He was lighting a cigarette, and as he raised his head their eyes met for a split second that, to Farrell, had something of the quality of a lightning flash about it. Because in that split second she saw with utter clarity that Larry *knew* Mark Nelson was the man she had 'run away' with. Had he known all the time? she wondered bewilderedly. Or—or what had she said that night she was unconscious? Her throat was dry, but she finished her tea and she felt incapable of either asking for, or getting herself, another cup.

'It's all arranged, is it?' There was a chill in Larry's voice that made Farrell shiver.

'Not quite,' said Helen. 'You see, they parted company—he apparently left her somewhere up the bush, just don't ask me where or why—but he was going back to ask her as soon as he'd had some repair job done on his car.'

'And he's sure she'll say yes?'

Farrell closed her eyes. She wanted to cry out that she would never say yes, that it was all crazy, but she stayed silent and helpless as if she were in the grip of some unending nightmare.

'Well, I should say so,' Helen said confidently. 'Girls have always liked Mark. And anyhow'—she sounded amused, tolerant—'I gather they're as good as married already. It's just a matter of making up their minds to do the good old-fashioned thing and make it legal.'

Oh God! It grew worse and worse. Farrell could feel Larry looking at her and as if compelled she raised her lashes. His eyes were smouldering. Their patent accusation seemed to burn through to her very soul. Only this morning he had said he believed what she had told him about herself and Mark. Now, quite simply, she wished she could die . . .

'You will help him, won't you, darling?' Helen murmured persuasively.

'I'm not making you any promises,' said Larry, his voice hard. 'If Marks wants any favours from me, he can plead his own case. I'll decide then what proposition I'll make him—if any.'

'Oh, Larry, you are hard,' Helen protested. 'You've always been so good about him before. I know he's given my parents all sorts of trouble and heartache, but he *is* my brother, and despite what happened to Brian, I could never turn my back on him or refuse to help. This could just be the one thing that's going to settle him down——'

There was a brief silence, then Helen said brightly, 'Poor Farrell! None of this makes any sense to you, does it? You look bored to tears—or are you feeling sick?'

Farrell *was* feeling sick. She murmured something to that effect and stumbled to her feet. 'Please excuse me,' she managed to say before she turned away and headed for the house.

'Are you all right, Farrell?' Larry's voice followed her.

'Quite all right,' she tossed back over her shoulder. 'I'll have a rest before dinner.'

She had been afraid he might follow her—hurl unanswerable accusations in her face—but he didn't. No, she thought, he won't bother about me any more. If only it had happened earlier—before she had discovered that she was in love with him!

In her room, she sat on the side of the bed, her face in her hands, waiting for her stomach to stop churning. She simply couldn't believe that Mark was coming to look for her—that he wanted her to marry him. It was so utterly fantastic that she almost wanted to laugh. Almost, but not quite, because it was not a mad dream, it was real. So what happened next? Would Mark find her? Where would he look? she wondered. Not at that roadhouse where they had spent their last night together—under the name of Mr and Mrs Smith. Then in Port Hedland, perhaps? Or would he do the more rational thing and ring through to her father's hotel? If Tony told him she was at Quindalup, then he could turn up here at any time . . .

'Farrell——'

She raised her head, startled, to find Helen had come into the room and was standing looking at her.

'I came to see how you're feeling. You look terrible. Why don't you get into bed? I'll tell Mrs Adams to bring you something on a tray—nobody will mind in the slightest if you don't come out to dinner.'

No, Farrell could well believe that. She noted abstractedly that Helen said 'Mrs Adams'—not 'my mother-in-law'. Larry had said they didn't have a close relationship.

'Come on,' Helen said briskly. 'Don't sit there looking like a stunned mullet. Shall I help you to undress?'

'No, thank you,' said Farrell, and was more than a little surprised to hear herself add, 'Your mother-in-law will help me if I need any assistance.'

Helen's lovely eyes were suddenly cold. 'You *are* intent on emphasising that—relationship, aren't you? I wonder why? *I* know a lot more about *you* than you imagine, by the way.'

Farrell, feeling sicker than ever, bent to take her shoes off. So Helen did know she was the girl who had come south with Mark. But why hadn't she already said so? She was about to ask when Helen swept on. 'Farrell Fitzgerald. I knew your name was familiar, and I've remembered why.'

'Why?' Farrell asked exhaustedly, fully expecting the answer to be linked up with Mark. But it wasn't.

'Because we've met before.' Helen sauntered over to the dressing table and looked at herself in the mirror, touching her dark hair, moistening her upper lip with her tongue. Then she turned back to Farrell. '*You* wouldn't remember. My mother and I spent a holiday up on the coast when I was a schoolgirl, and we put in a couple of nights at your father's scruffy hotel .... It's a small world, isn't it?'

Scruffy? Farrell's head was throbbing. Perhaps her father's hotel used to be a little scruffy—there wasn't much civilisation up there then. But things were different now. She wanted to tell Helen so, but she couldn't make the effort, and simply sat staring at her—and feeling somehow thankful that Helen didn't know about her association with Mark. She was coming very rapidly to the conclusion that she didn't much like 'lovely Helen'.

'Yes, well—I remember very clearly being absolutely horrified the way a little kid like you was allowed to hang around the bar with all the tough characters there. I was so protected.' She paused and smiled slightly, and Farrell absently began to turn her bed down. 'I suppose you grew up to work behind the bar and mix with the men. Larry must have been *very* different from the usual type. That's where you met him, isn't it?—when he was looking for my brother. How did you manage to scrounge an invitation to Quindalup? Or did you invite yourself? Anyhow, you can stop feasting your eyes on him now, the way you were doing this afternoon—because as it happens he's my property.'

'Is he?' Farrell's voice sounded blurred in her own ears. She felt terrible—she wished Helen would go away and leave her alone. All she wanted was to escape into sleep. She lay back on the bed, her head on the pillow, her eyes closed.

'Yes, he is. I've known him since I was a child. We were very close. But he's quite a few years older than I am, and because of that, I guess things didn't go the way they should have, the way he wanted them to. I married someone else. He was killed in a plane accident last year. I felt I'd never get over his death at the time—but I have. What we had was very sweet—and very young. I've grown up since, and I know now that deep inside I've always loved Larry. He's the man I should have married, and when he asks me, I'll say yes.'

Farrell opened her eyes and looked at her across the room.

'Hasn't he asked you yet?'

Helen gave a little smile. 'Farrell, Larry is a very sensitive, very proud person. Obviously, you scarcely know him or you'd realise that. If he felt my heart was still with Brian—still anchored to the past—he wouldn't ask a thing of me.'

Farrell stared at her, her heart thudding. She didn't like Helen, but that didn't prevent her from acknowledging that Helen's life was linked more intimately with Larry's than hers was. She and Larry *didn't* understand each other, knew next to nothing about one another. Once, Larry had meant to remedy that. Once, when he had thought there was no hope of Helen's ever belonging to him as he would want his wife to belong ...

'He knows how I feel now,' Helen said softly. 'We had a long talk in Perth, just recently.'

The day he left me at Quindalup, Farrell thought dully. She turned her face away from Helen's gaze. 'I think I'll get into bed now. I shan't come out to dinner.'

'That would be wise,' said Helen. She sounded smug. 'It will give Larry and me a chance to talk more freely, too. A third person always hampers the conversation when it's more or less—intimate. I'll see to it you get your tray.'

'Don't bother. I'm not hungry,' Farrell said faintly. But Helen didn't hear her. The door had already clicked shut behind her.

CHAPTER TEN

NUMBLY, Farrell got herself to bed. Her body was aching and so was her heart. For a long time she lay quite still, trying to make her mind a peaceful blank, trying to accept what she had to accept. She wished it was about a hundred years from now.

Someone knocked at the door. For a crazy moment she thought it might be Larry, but it was Mrs Adams with her dinner tray. Farrell thanked her and managed a smile, and after she had gone, picked uninterestedly at her food. Finally she put the tray aside and got out of bed to stand looking across the verandah into the darkness of the garden. She could smell sweet flower scents and she could hear soft music, the murmur of voices. Helen and Larry were having their heart-to-heart talk. Helen had recovered from the loss of Brian Adams, she was ready to marry Larry who had been waiting for her for—how many years? That birthday card, Farrell thought—he might have sent her that years ago.

Warm tears began to run down her cheeks, and choking back a sob she climbed back into bed and switched off the reading lamp. She felt sick and sore and sorry for herself, and her bruises were hurting. When, she didn't know how much later, someone called her name at the door she didn't answer. She saw a crack of light that widened as the door softly opened, and once again Larry's voice said, 'Farrell?'

Farrell lay quite still. She didn't want to be told what he thought of her—she didn't want to discuss Mark or anything at all. She didn't speak, and after a few seconds Larry closed the door and went away.

Mornings were always bringing surprises, not always pleasant ones, and the next morning was no exception. Before Farrell was even awake—and certainly she had slept exhaustedly and hadn't wakened till nearly ten—Helen and Larry had gone.

'To Mullamulla Downs,' Mrs Adams told her when she brought Farrell's breakfast into the bedroom. 'Helen asked me to say goodbye to you and say it was nice to have met you. Mr Sandfort wouldn't wake you. You need all the sleep you can get, he said. How are you feeling this morning, dear?'

'I feel fine,' said Farrell, who felt terrible. As well, she felt terribly deserted, terribly alone, terribly much in need of a shoulder to cry on. Someone to love her, someone to sympathise without asking questions. And she needed to be a long, long way away where Mark couldn't find her. And where Larry couldn't find her either. It was so ironical that he had planned to produce between them a kind of—factory-made love. Now *he* had no need of that kind of love, and as for Farrell—he had meanwhile, without even knowing it, stirred her to love, a love that was all too real. But that was something he would never know, and possibly never believe if he did know. His opinion of her now must be at an all-time low. She and Mark were 'as good as married already', Helen had said . . .

Suddenly Farrell felt she couldn't bear to see any of them ever again. Body and mind she was one big ache, and she wanted her father's arms around her. She had to get out of here.

She drank some coffee, ate a little of the toast and marmalade. Showered, dressed—packed. All as if she were making pre-considered moves. She was more concerned with the limitations placed on her by her bruised body than with what she was doing, and when she had finished packing, she looked at her suitcases in a kind of blank surprise.

How on earth did she think she was going to get away from Quindalup? And where was she going?

Home, of course. Home to her father, and damn Cecile's jealousy. She had to cry on somebody's shoulder and there was only Tony. Aunt Jean had no time for tears. And when she had cried and cried and cried, then perhaps she would have to go back to Perth—unless some other fabulous and intriguing man should materialise and beg her to marry him.

She heard herself laugh mirthlessly, and was aware she was slightly hysterical, and that the effort of dressing and packing had exhausted her. She was tempted to lie down on the bed, but instead she went out to the garden. The sun was hot and bright, and she had to close her eyes against it. Strangely, in the garden she discovered Mrs Adams' car— with the windows down, and the keys in the ignition. By the look of it, the housekeeper had not long finished washing and polishing it. Farrell's heart leaped. This could be her opportunity. She glanced around and found Mrs Adams was in the side garden, watering the flowers, and visible from where Farrell stood. So it was no go. But she was not giving up hope, and for the rest of the morning she kept watch, though the chance she was hoping for did not eventuate. But at least the keys were still there.

They were still there by mid-afternoon, at which time Mrs Adams set off for a walk into the gorge, looking for wildflowers.

Farrell, installed on a lounger under the poinciana tree, watched her go, nervily, and as soon as she was out of sight she went inside for her luggage. Ten minutes later she was driving down the gravel road towards Ansell. She'd stop at some roadhouse overnight, she decided, and telephone through to Larry at Mullamulla Downs in the morning and tell him what she'd done. Because it was a pretty awful thing to borrow someone's car like this, and she felt decidedly guilty about it, particularly as Mrs Adams had been so good to her.

As it happened, however, Farrell didn't reach a road-house that night. Some sixty kilometres beyond Ansell, and within sight of a sign announcing that petrol, meals and accommodation were just forty-three kilometres ahead, the car spluttered and stopped dead.

Farrell, who knew nothing about the mechanics of a car, stared around her helplessly. It seemed like the end of everything, particularly feeling as she did. Spinifex country stretched away into the distance wherever she looked. A few crows and a flock of galahs flew overhead against a sky fired gorgeously by the sunset. Soon, she realised with a slight feeling of panic, it would be dark.

What on earth was she to do?

The only possible answer seemed to be to spend the night in the car, an unattractive prospect to say the least of it. But it was unlikely anyone would come this way—she hadn't seen a single vehicle since leaving Ansell. With a deep feeling of despondency, she knew she should have filled up her petrol tank there, but she hadn't wanted to linger, and the gauge—evidently unreliable—had shown half full. Well, it was too late for regrets.

She looked around her once more. The sun was going down rapidly, the flat-topped ranges etched dark shapes against the fast fading sky, and now the birds had gone there was not a living creature to be seen. Yet these lands must be part of some pastoralist's sheep station. There could even be a homestead stuck away behind some rise in the ground. On the point of leaving the car to explore, Farrell changed her mind. She was in no condition for a long walk over rough ground, and suppose she made the effort and found nothing—what then? She would have to find her way back to the car in the dark, and in the mean-time, she could have missed out on help. Also it was just possible she might find Mrs Adams' car stripped. It did sometimes happen on these lonely outback roads when a car broke down and was left unattended.

Farrell shivered a little. No, there was nothing to be done but stay where she was and hope it would not be too long before she was rescued. At least she could get into the back seat and try to get some sleep.

Sleep wouldn't come however, she discovered. Her mind was too active first with thoughts of her plight, then with thoughts of Larry. What was he doing now? she wondered. Had he and Helen already told the Nelsons that they wanted to be married? Were they all perhaps drinking a toast to the future? That reminded Farrell that she was beginning to be very thirsty, and very uncomfortable as well. She would have to get out and stretch her limbs.

But before she could do so, lights appeared against the blackness of the landscape. Car lights. Not on the road, but obliquely to her right. Someone driving out from one of the sheep stations. Farrell's heart raced. Quickly, terrified that the driver might be heading in the other direction when he reached the road, and never even know of her plight, she scrambled out of the car, forgetting her aching limbs, opened the driver's door and switched on the headlights. She counted three, then switched them off—then on again. She repeated the performance several times and then—oh, the blessed relief!—found the car had turned down the road in her direction. Farrell dimmed the lights and leaned back in the seat thanking heaven. She had to be safe now ...

The headlights of the other car dazzled her and it was not until it had pulled up on the road ahead of her and the lights had been switched off that she recognised Larry Sandfort's Landrover.

Farrell felt too absolutely stunned to know whether she was dismayed or completely otherwise. She certainly felt quite faint.

In a few seconds Larry was standing staring in at her.

'What on earth are you doing here, Farrell? Where's Mrs Adams?'

Farrell stared around her wide-eyed, then suddenly realised what he meant.

'Oh—she's not here. I—I took the car.'

'What?' he exclaimed explosively. 'You're meant to be taking it easy, not racing round the countryside at the wheel of a motor. What's the idea?'

Farrell wanted to cry. Instead she bit her lip hard before she answered. 'I can't stay at Quindalup for ever. I was going home. To my father. At least,' she continued wildly, suddenly aware of the very flimsy nature of her plans, 'I was going to take the plane when I—when I got somewhere—civilised. But I—I think I've run out of petrol.'

'Don't ask me to sympathise.' He swung the door open. 'Move over. Let me see.'

Farrell complied, than sat silently while he made his tests, and finally pronounced her diagnosis correct.

'No fuel. You're out of action, Farrell. What are you going to do about it?'

She creased her forehead slightly. 'Where are *you* going, Larry?'

'Where do you think? But I won't give you three guesses. I'm going back to Quindalup, of course. I left a girl there.'

Farrell blinked and swallowed, uncertain of his mood. 'But—but what about Helen?'

'Well, what about her? To hell with Helen! Why talk about her?'

'Because—she talked about you.'

He looked at her sharply. 'Did she? And what did she say?'

'That now she's got over Brian's death, you'd want her to marry you.'

'And do you care?' he asked after a moment. Farrell,

who wished she had held her tongue, said nothing and he went on, 'It's nonsense, anyhow. Helen depends on her physical beauty to bring every man she meets to her feet, but lovely though she is, her attraction for me was never more than skin deep. I've known her since she was a child and she was vain and greedy even then. Now let's forget about her.'

'But you took her home to Mullamulla Downs. I'm sure she thought——'

'Farrell, I can't help what she thought. All I wanted was to get her out of the way. And I'd have been back at Quindalup long before this if Bob hadn't wanted me to go over some book work with him. Now for God's sake don't start being sorry for Helen—she doesn't lack for admirers in Perth, she can choose one of them any time she wants. I'm not all that important to her.'

'Oh,' said Farrell inadequately. She didn't agree with his last statement, but it was useless to argue, and she was still sorry for Helen. 'Anyhow,' she resumed, 'I didn't think you'd want to come to Quindalup—not while I was there.'

'Why not?' Larry had turned towards her and the light from the dash illumined his face sufficiently for her to see the blueness of his eyes, now fixed on her, and she was aware of a weak melting sensation that made her almost incapable of speech.

'I know what you think—that you're angry about me and Mark——' It was all she could manage, and it sounded guilty and terrible.

His eyes still considered her. 'I might be angry with Mark, Farrell, but I'm not angry with you. I told you I believed you—and I haven't changed my mind.'

A shiver went through her. 'But,' she said forlornly, 'you must have heard what Helen said——'

'Yes, I heard it, but I didn't believe it,' he said grimly. 'I'd have told you so last night, but you were asleep when I went to your room. So it had to wait until I'd come back from Mullamulla Downs ... You know, I'm only just beginning to realise how fortunate it was you did run out of petrol, Farrell. I suppose you didn't tell Mrs Adams where you were going. Did you leave her a letter?'

Farrell shook her head. She felt dazed, bewildered. Larry didn't believe what Helen had said about her and Mark being as good as married! It didn't seem possible. She had seen the anger in his eyes—she had been so sure of his contempt. 'I was going to telephone them—at Mullamulla Downs in the morning. From a roadhouse. About the car,' she said somewhat incoherently.

He nodded thoughtfully. 'Who were you running away from? Mark? Or were you expecting to catch up with him at your father's place?'

'No,' she said quickly. 'I don't want to see Mark. I—I can't believe he wants to marry me.'

She saw him smile crookedly. 'I can believe it. With no effort at all ... Are you interested? Do you want to marry him?'

'No!' she repeated briefly and vehemently.

'Well, that certainly sounds definite enough ... Where do you want me to take you, Farrell? Are you still determined on going home to your father? Or will you come back with me to Quindalup?'

Farrell had no idea what to say. Of course she wanted to go back with him to Quindalup, but she was badly confused. She was afraid to examine the stirring of hope in her heart, in case it vanished. Yet Larry had said he believed her—and he had said he wasn't going to marry Helen. Oh, if only they could go back to the beginning and start all over again with that original proposition of his, how happy she would be!

'Perhaps you want to run away from me too,' he said soberly, when she didn't answer. 'I'm painfully aware that I haven't behaved in a way to make you feel exactly enamoured of me, but I'd like a chance to alter that.'

Farrell drew a deep slow breath and turned slightly to face him. He was wrong in thinking she wasn't enamoured of him. She was hopelessly so—and she longed for him to know it. Her lips parted, but she couldn't speak.

'Do you think I could alter it?' he asked after a second. 'Because I love you, Farrell ... Dementedly,' he added beneath his breath, and reached for her. Dizzily, meltingly, she let herself be pulled into his arms, and she had a crazy feeling she must be delirious. Because it just wasn't possible that he could love her, dementedly or otherwise. Though after a few minutes of being held closely against his body, with his mouth exploring hers, she was convinced otherwise.

'You see?' he said when, reluctantly, he let her go so they could both regain their breath. 'I think maybe—just maybe—I could teach you to love me. You're a very promising pupil. Will you come to Quindalup and do that crash course we talked about once?'

He was smiling at her and Farrell rested one hand flat on his chest as she looked back at him. She could feel his warmth, feel the strong steady beating of his heart, and she was ready to die of love.

'I'd like it,' she said huskily.

'You would? Then you're an angel. I know I don't deserve it—that I've been unbearable. I can only excuse myself by repeating that unfortunately I'm a romantic—that I'm out of tune with the times, with Women's Lib and sexual freedom—the lot. Do you know, it made me see red when I thought you'd had a lover. I almost imagined I could hate you—and certainly I wanted to kill him. The trouble was I didn't hate you—I loved you—and I wanted to be the one to teach you about love——'

'You have, Larry,' she murmured, raising her face to his

and linking her hands provocatively behind his neck. She remembered with amazement her fears that she was frightened of passion and incapable of it herself. In Larry's arms, she knew that was nonsense.

'Darling, I haven't taught you a thing yet,' he protested. 'But don't provoke me—this isn't the time or the place and I really think we'd better get moving. There are much more satisfactory places for making love.' His voice was rueful and Farrell saw the gleam of his teeth as he smiled at her and her heart thudded. Reluctantly she moved away from him.

He locked up Mrs Adams' car, murmured something about sending someone out from Ansell for it, then installed her in the front seat of the Landrover, and they were on their way.

In five minutes Farrell was exhaustedly asleep, though she would much sooner have stayed awake so she could savour what Larry had said. 'I love you dementedly.'

When she opened her eyes, she was sure it was somethng she had dreamed, it wasn't real, it couldn't be. She glanced at the man beside her to assure herself it really was Larry, then caught her breath at the feelings the mere sight of him aroused in her. He turned and smiled at her, and she smiled back. She realised they were in Ansell, driving along a tree-lined street that smelled of orange blossoms and jasmine and pittosporum flowers—of all the sweet flowers of spring, the air was still warm, and a small silver moon had floated into the sky among the stars.

'Feeling better?' Larry asked. 'I think we'll stop here, Farrell. You've had about all you can take for one day, and I guess we both need a meal. All right?'

She nodded, too happy to speak. But as he pulled up in his own particular parking spot at the motel and reached for her suitcases, she suddenly thought of Mark and felt a pang. Meeting him again was not going to be altogether pleasant. She just couldn't imagine how she would sort all that out, but oh, she mustn't think about it now and spoil everything. She would wait till it happened.

In the motel she waited while Larry got his keys, and when he turned away from the desk and came towards her and their eyes met, she thought she could look into the blueness of his for ever. They went straight to his suite and when he had dropped her suitcases on the floor, he pulled her into his arms and kissed her again, with restrained passion. Then holding her a little away from him, he drew a finger down the line of her cheek. 'We'd better go in to dinner, Farrell. Don't worry about changing your clothes —you don't look as if you could stand it, you're like a drooping flower. God knows what your father would say if he could see you now. He'd never trust you to my care again—and seeing I hope to marry you that would never do, would it?'

'I'm all right,' she said, smiling. 'Really, Larry. I slept— I feel wonderful. Just a bit hungry.'

In the little dressing room she splashed water on her face and combed her hair, and though her face was pale with fatigue there were stars in her eyes that simply couldn't be extinguished.

They shared a light meal in the dining room, sitting at a secluded table, speaking very little and staring into each other's eyes like lovers. Farrell thought of Quindalup—how soon they would be walking up the gorge to the lily ponds, swimming together in the pool near the sun shelter, relaxing on the li-los under the trees and telling each other everything. It wasn't going to take her a week or even a day to decide whether or not she would marry him. She knew the answer now, and she knew that she would be quite ready for him to teach her all about love. She was afraid of nothing.

As they left the dining room and strolled along the terrace outside the cocktail bar, her glance went lazily over the crowd sitting at the tables. She remembered as if it belonged to another world that handsome boy who had stared at her when she had been here before, then suddenly she discovered someone was staring at her. She stiffened. Seated at the end of one of the tables was Mark. Farrell's face went white with shock. She had known she would have to face him some time, but not tonight. Tonight was too soon—she couldn't cope. Larry's arm was lightly around her shoulders and she drew some comfort from that. She prayed Mark wouldn't bluff his way through some frightful scene that she would find impossible to handle—that he wasn't going to manage to spoil everything now it had come right. More than ever she was convinced he must merely be planning to use her as a convincing argument that he was really ready to settle down. Yet how could he do that? Especially now she was here with Larry. He surely couldn't pick an argument—he knew very well she had no sentimental feelings for him. She simply couldn't understand it, and the confusion of her thoughts was making her feel ill.

Now Mark was on his feet, a smile on his good-looking face, signalling to her and to Larry.

'Hi, Larry—Farrell!' Larry paused and Farrell paused too, her limbs trembling, while Mark came jauntily towards them. 'You're just the person I hoped to see,' he told Larry with a grin. He turned his head. 'Hey, Ruth, come and be introduced.'

Farrell stared as a tall red-haired girl in jeans and a blue cotton shirt embroidered with big flowers rose from the table and came forward obligingly.

'Ruth, this is Larry Sandfort—I was telling you about him. Oh, and Farrell Fitzgerald. This is Ruth, my fiancée. Ruth Howard. I guess you're not really surprised, Larry. Helen said she'd break the ice for me ... Ruth and I saw a lot of each other about six months ago, and we met up again just recently in Meekatharra. She's the reason I've decided to quit the roving life and settle down to be a married man.'

Farrell felt almost too stunned to take it all in. So this was the girl Mark wanted to marry! It wasn't her at all. It was such an immense relief she wanted to laugh. She didn't know if she said anything at all, but she was vaguely aware of Larry offering his congratulations and adding coolly, 'Yes, Helen gave us the news in a general sort of way. I believe you have ideas about working for Ansell-Sandfort Mining.'

'Yair,' Mark agreed. 'Join us for a drink, will you, and we can talk about it. Let's find a table to ourselves.' He turned around and reached for a nearby chair and pulled it out. 'Sit down, Farrell. It's great to see you again. And by the way,' he added looking back at Larry, 'Ruth here would like a job too.'

'I rather thought she might,' Larry said dryly. He had put a hand on Farrell's arm, restraining her as she moved unwillingly towards the seat Mark offered. 'Well, I'm not going to talk about it tonight. You'll have to wait till it's more convenient—and till I've given the matter some thought. If I do offer you a job, I'm not going to promise it will be something you'll rush. You'll have to make the best of what's available, or look elsewhere.' Then, with a brief smile at Ruth, he wished them both goodnight, and taking Farrell by the arm, guided her past the tables in the direction of his rooms.

Farrell didn't find her voice till they were inside with the door shut behind them. Then she asked frowningly, '*Aren't* you going to offer Mark work, Larry? You sounded so—hard.'

'I was feeling hard,' he said, pulling her down on the settee beside him and putting his arm around her shoulders. 'To tell the truth, it was all I could do not to king-hit that young fellow.'

Farrell's lips parted on a gasp. She had thought Mark

might cause a scene—but it seemed Larry had been the one more likely to do that! 'But—but *why*?'

'Because he needs to be taught a lesson.'

'I don't understand. Those things he told Helen—they were about Ruth, not me. She looks quite nice,' she added inconsequentially. 'Mark didn't do me any harm, Larry. You've already said you believed that.'

'Oh yes, I believe it to some extent.' He pulled her against him and brushed his lips lightly across her mouth and she felt a tremor of desire go through her. 'You'd better hurry up and get youself up to that hundred per cent standard of fitness pretty soon, Farrell,' he said under his breath, tangling his fingers in her soft curling hair, his blue eyes exploring her grey-green ones. 'What did happen between you, anyhow, Farrell? I know there was some-thing—you were having quite a struggle that night you were delirious, and that was when you began to mutter about Mark Nelson. You might as well tell me now. I don't want to spend the whole of my married life wondering, and I'd sooner hear it here than at Quindalup.'

Colour flooded her face, then subsided again. It still upset her to remember that night at the roadhouse, and even now she knew she couldn't bring herself to tell the whole of it to Larry. 'Nothing happened really,' she said after a moment. 'I know now that I asked for trouble careering off with Mark the way I did—I asked him to let me come, you see. I was just too stupid to realise he'd—expect anything of me.'

Larry raised his eyebrows. 'Not too stupid. Too inno-cent, perhaps.'

'Well—I suppose so,' she conceded. 'Anyhow, everything was all right at first and then that last night he—he tried to start something.' She bit her lip, then forced herself to go on. 'He'd always just—got into his own bed, before, but this time he—he wanted to get into mine. So I screamed and—he just left me alone,' she concluded, thinking how terrible it all sounded. 'It was very decent of him really, wasn't it, though, Larry? I mean, he could have made things very awkward, but he didn't, so it's really not fair if you take it out on him by not giving him a chance.'

Larry's eyes were dark and he was scowling. 'For God's sake,' he exclaimed, 'you don't expect me to praise him for his consideration, do you? I still say he deserves a good punch on the jaw!'

'But nothing happened,' Farrell insisted, a little alarmed by the look in his eyes.

'Nothing happened? Didn't he drop you off alone and defenceless bang in the middle of what's decidedly a man's country? If nothing happened *then*, it was certainly not his fault ... Come to think of it,' he added after a moment, and now the line of his mouth had softened in a way she loved, 'it's possibly Mark's fault we're here together now—sharing this VIP unit in the mining town of Ansell, W.A. In fact, you're now in a *very* dangerous situation, Farrell, because I'm not taking you back to Quindalup till tomorrow. Have you any objections?'

'None,' said Farrell. Her eyes met his laughingly, and then suddenly they were both very serious, and as Larry pulled her to him she knew the utmost bliss. This was what she had come a thousand miles to find—love in the arms of the man she adored, the beginning of a new and thrilling adventure.

Masquerade
Historical Romances

Stories full of intrigue,
excitement and romance....
Woven from history's rich tapestry of life, love
and adventure, each novel in the Masquerade
Historical Romance series emphasizes
the timelessness of love through the ages.
You, too, can be transported back to a bygone
age of true romance, when deeds were daring
and heroes dashing and the smile of
a beautiful woman could change the course
of history anywhere in the world....

Masquerade titles are now being
published every month.

July Titles

SOPHIE AND THE PRINCE
Sylvia Sark
The sweet and gentle Sophie
Johnson travels to pre-revolutionary
Russia to be English teacher to the
daughters of the dynamic Prince
Peter Rasimov. There she falls
deeply in love with him, but
wonders how she can overcome the
difference in their backgrounds and
deal with the treachery of the
scheming French governess.

THE DEVIL'S DAUGHTER
Marguerite Bell
As companion to his wards, Harriet
Yorke does not hesitate to confront
the Marquis of Capel when he
neglects them. Her appearance at
the scene of a duel almost causes
his death, but gentle nursing does
nothing to make her obstinate
patient alter his low opinion of her.
Is jealousy the answer?

MADELON
Valentina Luellen
Returning to court in 11th century
Spain the beautiful Madelon and
her brother Paco are captured by
fierce Moors. Almost enslaved,
their rescue comes unexpectedly
from the noble and magnificent
Valentin Maratin, her brother's
sworn enemy...

STRANGER AT THE GATE
Frances Lang
After years of exile in Holland,
Clemence de Frainville's brother
unexpectedly returns to his family
château in France. Clemence is
initially puzzled when she does not
recognise Edouard, and then
angered when he forbids her to
marry the handsome Armand.

Order your copies now and be among the first
to enter our exciting world of historical romance

OLD-FASHIONED VALUE AT 60p net.

DON'T MISS JULY'S
GREAT DOCTOR - NURSE ROMANCES

NURSE IN TENERIFE *by Pippa Lane*
Nurse Trudy Forrest was not happy when she had
to leave her beloved Derek to nurse her stepmother on the island of Tenerife. She was even
less happy when she met Miguel Martina, the handsome Spanish surgeon, who told her he had fallen
in love with her even before they met . . .

HOLIDAY HOSPITAL *by Juliet Shore*
Her job as a surgeon was the only thing that
mattered to Amanda Verne when she arrived in
Majorca — but Doctor Vicente, the aristocratic
Spaniard, was determined to change her mind, and
so was Luke Hallward, the head of the hospital.
But another woman was determined to marry
Luke, by fair means or foul!

**LOOK OUT FOR THEM AT YOUR NEAREST
MILLS & BOON STOCKIST** Only 50p